EX LIBRIS

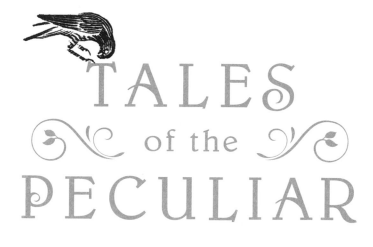

TALES of the PECULIAR

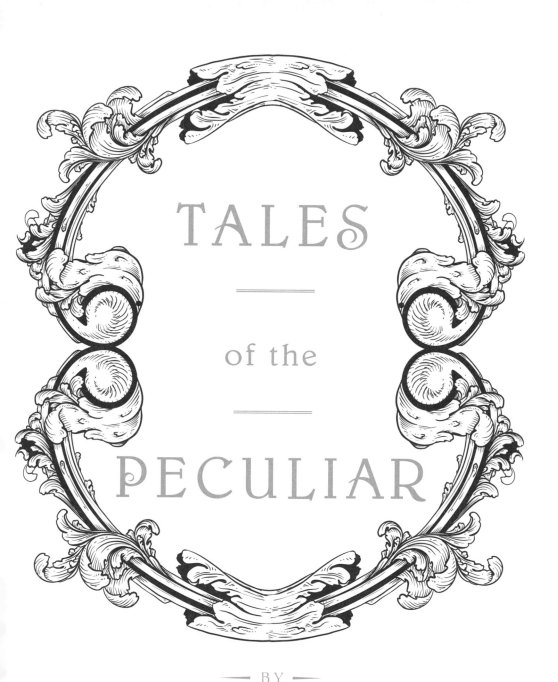

TALES

— of the —

PECULIAR

— BY —

MILLARD NULLINGS

ILLUSTRATIONS BY ANDREW DAVIDSON

SYNDRIGAST PUBLICATIONS

TALES of the PECULIAR
Edited and annotated by Millard Nullings
Illustrated by Andrew Davidson

To Alma LeFay Peregrine, who taught me to love tales

—MN

Homo sum: humani nil a me alienum puto.

—Terence

Dear Reader,

The book you hold in your hands is meant for peculiar eyes only. If by chance you are not among the ranks of the anomalous—in other words, if you don't find yourself floating out of bed in the middle of the night because you forgot to tie yourself to the mattress, sprouting flames from the palms of your hands at inopportune times, or chewing food with the mouth in the back of your head—then please put this book back where you found it at once and forget this ever happened. Don't worry, you won't be missing anything. I'm sure you'd only find the stories contained herein strange, distressing, and altogether not to your liking. And anyway, they're none of your business.

Very peculiarly yours,

The Publisher

FOREWORD

I F YOU ARE OF THE PECULIAR PERSUASION— and if you've read this far, I sincerely hope that you are— then this is a book that likely needs no introduction. These tales were a formative and beloved part of your upbringing, and you came of age reading them and hearing them read aloud with such frequency that you can recite your favorites word for word. If, however, you are among those unfortunates who have only just discovered their peculiarity, or who grew up in circumstances where no peculiar literature was available, I offer this brief primer.

TALES of the PECULIAR is a collection of our most beloved folklore. Passed down from generation to generation since time immemorial, each story is part history, part fairy tale, and part moral lesson aimed at young peculiars. These tales hail from various parts of the globe, from oral as well as written traditions, and have gone through striking transformations over the years. They have survived as long as they have because they are loved for their merits as stories, but they are more than that, too. They are also the bearers of secret knowledge. Encoded within their pages are the locations of hidden loops, the secret identities of certain important peculiars, and other information that could aid a peculiar's survival in this hostile world. I should know: the

Tales are the reason I'm alive to write these words now. They preserved not only my life, but those of my friends and our beloved ymbryne. I, Millard Nullings, am a living testament to the enduring usefulness of these stories, though they were written many years ago.

That's why I've devoted myself to their preservation and dissemination, and taken it upon myself to edit and annotate this special edition of the *Tales*. It is by no means exhaustive or complete—the edition I grew up reading was a famously unwieldy three-volume set that weighed, collectively, more than my friend Bronwyn—but the stories contained here represent my very favorites, and I have taken the liberty of annotating them with historical and contextual insights so that peculiars everywhere may benefit from my wisdom. It's also my hope that this edition, being more portable than previous ones, will be an easy companion on your travels and adventures, and may prove itself as useful to you as it once did to me.

So please enjoy these *Tales*—before a crackling fire on a chilly night, ideally, a snoring grimbear at your feet—but remember, too, their sensitive nature, and if you must read them aloud (which I highly recommend) make certain your audience is peculiar.

Millard Nullings

—*Millard Nullings, Esq., EdD, MBCh*

The Splendid Cannibals

he peculiars in the village of Swampmuck lived very modestly. They were farmers, and though they didn't own fancy things and lived in flimsy houses made of reeds, they were healthy and joyful and wanted for little. Food grew bountifully in their gardens, clean water ran in the streams, and even their humble homes seemed like luxuries because the weather in Swampmuck was so fair, and the villagers were so devoted to their work that many, after a long day of mucking, would simply lie down and sleep in their swamps.

Harvest was their favorite time of year. Working round the clock, they gathered the best weeds that had grown in the swamp that season, bundled them onto donkey carts, and drove their bounty to the market town of Chipping Whippet, a five days' ride, to sell what they could. It was difficult work. The swampweed was rough and tore their hands. The donkeys were ill-tempered and apt to bite. The road to market was pitted with holes and plagued by thieves. There were often grievous accidents, such as when Farmer Pullman, in a fit of overzealous harvesting, accidentally scythed off his neighbor's leg. The neighbor, Farmer

Hayworth, was understandably upset, but the villagers were such agreeable people that all was soon forgiven. The money they earned at market was paltry but enough to buy necessities and some rations of goat-rump besides, and with that rare treat as their centerpiece they threw a raucous festival that went on for days.

That very year, just after the festival had ended and the villagers were about to return to their toil in the swamps, three visitors arrived. Swampmuck rarely had visitors of any kind, as it was not the sort of place people wanted to visit, and it had certainly never had visitors like these: two men and a lady dressed head to toe in lush brocaded silk, riding on the backs of three fine Arabian horses. But though the visitors were obviously rich, they looked emaciated and swayed weakly in their bejeweled saddles.

The villagers gathered around them curiously, marveling at their beautiful clothes and horses.

"Don't get too close!" Farmer Sally warned. "They look as if they might be sick."

"We're on a journey to the coast of Meek,"[1] explained one of the visitors, a man who seemed to be the only one strong enough to speak. "We were accosted by bandits some weeks ago and, though we were able to outrun them, we got badly lost. We've been turning circles ever since, looking for the old Roman Road."

"You're nowhere near the Roman Road," said Farmer Sally.

"Or the coast of Meek," said Farmer Pullman.

"How far is it?" the visitor asked.

"Six days' ride," answered Farmer Sally.

---

1. An historic zone of exile thought to lie somewhere within modern-day Cornwall.

"We'll never make it," the man said darkly.

At that, the silk-robed lady slumped in her saddle and fell to the ground.

The villagers, moved to compassion despite their concerns about disease, brought the fallen lady and her companions into the nearest house. They were given water and made comfortable in beds of straw, and a dozen villagers crowded around them offering help.

"Give them space!" said Farmer Pullman. "They're exhausted; they need rest!"

"No, they need a doctor!" said Farmer Sally.

"We aren't sick," the man said. "We're hungry. Our supplies ran out over a week ago, and we haven't had a bite to eat since then."

Farmer Sally wondered why such wealthy people hadn't simply bought food from fellow travelers on the road, but she was too polite to ask. Instead, she ordered some village boys to run and fetch bowls of swampweed soup and millet bread and what little goat-rump was left over from the festival—but when it was laid before the visitors, they turned the food away.

"I don't mean to be rude," said the man, "but we can't eat this."

"I know it's a humble spread," said Farmer Sally, "and you're probably used to feasts fit for kings, but it's all we have."

"It isn't that," the man said. "Grains, vegetables, animal meat—our bodies simply can't process them. And if we force ourselves to eat, it will only make us weaker."

The villagers were confused. "If you can't eat grains, vegetables, or animals," asked Farmer Pullman, "then what *can* you eat?"

"People," the man replied.

Everyone in the small house took a step back from the visitors.

"You mean to tell us you're . . . *cannibals*?" said Farmer Hayworth.

"By nature, not by choice," the man replied. "But, yes."

He went on to reassure the shocked villagers that they were civilized cannibals and never killed innocent people. They, and others like them, had worked out an arrangement with the king by which they agreed never to kidnap and eat people against their will, and in turn they were allowed to purchase, at terrific expense, the severed limbs of accident victims and the bodies of hanged criminals. This composed the entirety of their diet. They were now on their way to the coast of Meek because it was the place in Britain that boasted both the highest rate of accidents and the most deaths by hanging, and so food was relatively abundant—if not exactly plentiful.

Even though cannibals in those days were wealthy, they nearly always went hungry; firmly law-abiding, they were doomed to live lives of perpetual undernourishment, forever tormented by an appetite they could rarely satisfy. And it seemed that the cannibals who had arrived in Swampmuck, already starving and many days from Meek, were now doomed to die.

Having learned all this, the people of any other village, peculiar or otherwise, would have shrugged their shoulders and let the cannibals starve. But the Swampmuckians were compassionate almost to a fault, and so no one was surprised when Farmer Hayworth took a step forward, hobbling on crutches, and said, "It just so happens that I lost my leg in an accident a few days ago. I tossed it into the swamp, but I'm sure I could find it again, if the eels haven't eaten it yet."

The cannibals' eyes brightened.

"You would do that?" the cannibal woman said, brushing long hair back from a skeletal cheek.

"I admit it feels a little strange," Hayworth said, "but we can't just let you die."

The other villagers agreed. Hayworth hobbled to the swamp and found his leg, fought off the eels that were nibbling at it, and brought it to the cannibals on a platter.

One of the cannibal men handed Hayworth a purse of money.

"What's this?" asked Hayworth.

"Payment," the cannibal man said. "The same amount the king charges us."

"I can't accept this," said Hayworth, but when he tried to return the purse, the cannibal put his hands behind his back and smiled.

"It's only fair," the cannibal said. "You've saved our lives!"

The villagers turned away politely as the cannibals began to eat. Farmer Hayworth opened the purse, looked inside, and turned a bit pale. It was more money than he'd ever seen in his life.

The cannibals spent the next few days eating and recovering their strength, and when they were finally ready to set off again for the coast of Meek—this time with good directions—the villagers all gathered to wish them good-bye. When the cannibals saw Farmer Hayworth, they noticed he was walking without the aid of crutches.

"I don't understand!" said one of the cannibal men, astounded. "I thought we ate your leg!"

"You did!" said Hayworth. "But when the peculiars of Swamp-muck lose their limbs, they grow them back again."[2]

2. There was a time—a certain long ago halcyon era—when peculiars could live together, unlooped and in the open, without fear of persecution. Peculiars of the day often divided themselves into groups according to their ability, a practice now frowned upon as it encourages tribalism and inter-peculiar hostility.

The cannibal got a funny look on his face, seemed about to say more, then thought better of it. And he got on his horse and rode away with the others.

Weeks passed. Life in Swampmuck returned to normal for everyone but Farmer Hayworth. He was distracted, and during the day he could often be found leaning on his mucking stick, gazing out over the swamps. He was thinking about the purse of money, which he'd hidden in a hole. What should he do with it?

His friends all made suggestions.

"You could buy a wardrobe of beautiful clothes," said Farmer Bettelheim.

"But what would I do with them?" Farmer Hayworth replied. "I work in the swamps all day; they would only get ruined."

"You could buy a library of fine books," suggested Farmer Hegel.

"But I can't read," replied Hayworth, "and neither can anyone in Swampmuck."

Farmer Bachelard's suggestion was silliest of all. "You should buy an elephant," he said, "and use it to haul all your swampweed to market."

"But it would *eat* all the swampweed before I could sell it!" said Hayworth, becoming exasperated. "If only I could do something about my house. The reeds do little to keep the wind out, and it gets drafty in the winter."

"You could use the money to paper the walls," said Farmer Anderson.

"Don't be an idiot," Farmer Sally piped up. "Just buy a new house!"

And that's exactly what Hayworth did: he built a house made of wood, the first ever constructed in Swampmuck. It was small but sturdy and kept out the wind, and it even had a door that swung open and shut on hinges. Farmer Hayworth was very proud, and his house was the envy of the entire village.

Some days later, another group of visitors arrived. There were four of them, three men and a woman, and because they were dressed in fine clothes and rode on Arabian horses, the villagers knew right away who they were—law-abiding cannibals from the coast of Meek.[3] These cannibals, however, did not appear to be starving.

Again the villagers gathered round to marvel at them. The cannibal woman, who wore a shirt spun with gold thread, pants buttoned with pearls, and boots trimmed with fox fur, said: "Friends of ours came to your village some weeks ago, and you showed them great kindness. Because we are not a people accustomed to kindness, we have come to thank you in person."

And the cannibals got down from their horses and bowed to the villagers, then went about shaking the villagers' hands. The villagers were amazed at the softness of the cannibals' skin.

"One more thing before we go!" said the cannibal woman. "We heard you have a unique talent. Is it true you regrow lost limbs?"

The villagers told them it was true.

"In that case," the woman said, "we have a modest proposal for you. The limbs we eat on the coast of Meek are rarely fresh, and we're tired of rotten food. Would you sell us some of yours? We would pay handsomely, of course."

She opened her saddlepack to reveal a wad of money and jewels.

---

3. The source of the cannibals' wealth? The manufacture of candy and children's toys.

The villagers goggled at the money, but they felt uncertain and turned away to whisper amongst themselves.

"We can't sell our limbs," Farmer Pullman reasoned. "I need my legs for walking!"

"Then only sell your arms," said Farmer Bachelard.

"But we need our arms for swamp-mucking!" said Farmer Hayworth.

"If we're being paid for our arms, we won't need to grow swamp-weed anymore," said Farmer Anderson. "We hardly earn anything from farming, anyway."

"It doesn't seem right, selling ourselves that way," said Farmer Hayworth.

"Easy for you to say!" said Farmer Bettelheim. "You've got a house made of wood!"

And so the villagers made a deal with the cannibals: those who were right-handed would sell their left arms, and those who were left-handed would sell their right arms, and they'd keep on selling them as they grew back. That way they'd have a steady source of income and would never again have to spend all day mucking or endure a difficult harvest. Everyone seemed pleased with the arrangement except Farmer Hayworth, who rather enjoyed swamp-mucking, and was sorry to see the village give up its traditional trade, even if it wasn't very profitable compared to selling one's limbs to cannibals.

But there was nothing Farmer Hayworth could do, and he watched helplessly as all his neighbors gave up farming, let their swamps go fallow, and hacked their arms off. (Their peculiarity was such that it didn't hurt much, and the limbs came off rather easily, like a lizard's tail.) They used the money they earned to buy food from the market at Chipping

8

Whippet—goat-rump became a dish eaten daily rather than annually— and to build houses made of wood, like Farmer Hayworth's. Everyone wanted a door that swung on hinges, of course. Then Farmer Pullman built a house with two floors, and soon everyone wanted a house with two floors. Then Farmer Sally built a house with two floors *and* a gabled roof, and soon everyone wanted houses with two floors and a gabled roof. Every time the villagers' arms regrew and were hacked off and sold again, they would use the money to add to their houses. Finally the houses grew so big that there was hardly any room between them, and the village square, once wide and open, was reduced to a narrow alley.

Farmer Bachelard was the first one to hit upon a solution. He would buy a big plot of land on the outskirts of the village and build a new house there, even larger than his current one (which had, incidentally, three doors that swung on hinges, two floors, a gabled roof, *and* a porch). This was around the time when the villagers stopped going by "Farmer this" and "Farmer that" and started calling themselves "Mister this" and "Mrs. that," because they were no longer farmers—except for Farmer Hayworth, who kept on mucking his swamp and refused to sell any more limbs to the cannibals. He liked his simple house just fine, he insisted, and didn't even use it that much because he still enjoyed sleeping in his swamp after a hard day's work. His friends thought him silly and old-fashioned, and stopped coming by to see him.

The once-humble village of Swampmuck expanded rapidly as villagers bought larger and larger tracts of land upon which they built larger and more ornate houses. To finance this, they began selling the cannibals both an arm *and* a leg (the leg always on the opposite side from the arm, to make balancing easier), and learned to get around on crutches. The cannibals, whose hunger and wealth both seemed inexhaustible,

9

were very happy with this. Then Mister Pullman tore down his wooden house and replaced it with one made of brick, which touched off a race amongst the villagers to see who could build the grandest brick house. But Mister Bettelheim bested them all: he built a beautiful house made of honey-colored limestone, the sort of home only the richest merchants in Chipping Whippet lived in. He had afforded it by selling his arm and *both* of his legs.

"He's gone too far!" complained Mrs. Sally over goat-rump sandwiches in the fancy new restaurant the village had built.

Her friends agreed.

"How does he plan to enjoy his three-floor house," said Mrs. Wannamaker, "if he can't even walk up the stairs?"

It was just at that moment that Mister Bettelheim came into the restaurant—carried by a burly man from the neighboring village. "I've hired a man to carry me up and down the stairs, and anywhere else I want to go," he said proudly. "I don't need legs!"

The ladies were astounded. But soon they had sold their legs, too, and all across the village brick houses were being torn down and replaced by giant houses made of limestone.

The cannibals, by this time, had abandoned the coast of Meek to live in the forest near Swampmuck. There was no point anymore in subsisting on a meager diet of hanged criminals and accident victims' limbs when the villagers' limbs were fresher, tastier, and more plentiful than anything available in Meek. Their forest homes were modest because they gave so much of their money to the villagers, but the cannibals were nevertheless content, much happier to live in huts with full bellies than to go hungry in mansions.

As the villagers and the cannibals came to depend on one another, the appetites of each continued to grow. The cannibals became fat. Having exhausted every recipe they had for arms and legs, they began to wonder what the villagers' ears tasted like. But the villagers would not sell them their ears, because ears did not grow back. That is until Mister Bachelard, carried in the arms of his burly servant, paid a secret visit to the cannibals' forest and asked them how much they'd be willing to pay. He'd still be able to hear without his ears, he reasoned, and though it would make him a bit ugly, the fine house of white marble he'd be able to construct with the proceeds would be beautiful enough to compensate. (Now, the financially astute among you may be asking: why didn't Mister Bachelard just save up money from the ongoing sale of his arms and legs until he could afford a marble house? It's because he *couldn't* save money, because he'd taken out a very large loan from a bank in order to buy the land upon which his limestone house was built, and now he owed the bank an arm and a leg every month just to pay interest on the loan. So, he needed to sell his ears.)

The cannibals offered Mister Bachelard an exorbitant sum. Mister Bachelard snipped off his ears, happy to be rid of them, and replaced his limestone house with the marble home of his dreams. It was the most beautiful house in the village, and perhaps in all of Oddfordshire. Though the villagers of Swampmuck talked behind Bachelard's back about how ugly he'd made himself and how foolish it was to sell ears that would never grow back, they all paid him visits and had their servants carry them through the marble rooms and up and down the marble staircases, and by the time they left, each was green with envy.

By this time, none of the villagers but Farmer Hayworth had legs, and very few had arms. For a while they all insisted on keeping one arm so that they could point at things and feed themselves, but then they realized

11

that a servant could lift a spoon or a glass to their lips just as easily, and it was not much more trouble to say "fetch this for me" or "fetch that for me" than to point across a room at something. So arms became seen as needless luxuries, and the villagers, reduced to limbless torsos, would travel from place to place in silken sacks slung across their servants' shoulders.

Ears soon went the way of arms. The villagers pretended they had not called Mister Bachelard ugly.

"He doesn't look so bad," said Mister Bettelheim.

"We could wear earmuffs," suggested Mister Anderson.

And so their ears were snipped and sold, and marble houses were built. The village gained a reputation for its architectural beauty, and what had once been a backwater visited only by accident became a tourist destination. A hotel was built and several more restaurants. Goat-rump sandwiches were not even on the menu. The people of Swampmuck pretended they had never even *heard* of goat-rump sandwiches.

Tourists sometimes lingered near Farmer Hayworth's modest, flat-roofed house of wood, curious about the contrast between his simple home and the palaces that surrounded it. He would explain that he preferred the simple life of a four-limbed swampweed farmer and show them around his patch of swamp. His was the last bit of swamp in Swampmuck, as all the others had been filled in with dirt to make room for houses.

The eyes of the country were on Swampmuck and its beautiful marble homes. The homes' owners loved the attention but were desperate to stand out in some way, as every house was nearly identical. Each wanted to be known as the owner of the most beautiful house in Swampmuck, but they were already using their arms and legs every month just to pay interest on their enormous loans, and they had already sold their ears.

They began to approach the cannibals with new ideas.

"Would you loan me money with my nose as collateral?" asked Mrs. Sally.

"No," the cannibals said, "but we would happily buy your nose outright."

"But if I cut my nose off I'll look like a monster!" she said.

"You could wear a scarf around your face," they suggested.

Mrs. Sally refused, and from her sack she instructed her servant to take her home.

Next Mister Bettelheim came to see the cannibals.

"Would you buy my nephew?" he whispered, his servant pushing an eight-year-old boy before the cannibals.

"Absolutely not!" the cannibals replied, and gave the terrified boy a candy before sending him home.

Mrs. Sally returned a few days later. "Okay," she said with a sigh. "I'll sell you my nose."

She had it replaced with a false one made of gold and, with the money she earned, built an enormous gold dome on top of her marble house.

You may have guessed where this is going. The whole village sold their noses and built gold domes and turrets and towers. Then they sold their eyes—just one each—and used the money to dig moats around their houses, which they filled with wine and exotic, drunken fish. They said that binocular vision was a luxury anyway and needed mainly for throwing and catching things which, lacking arms, they didn't do anymore. And it only took one eye to appreciate the beauty of their homes.

Now, the cannibals were civilized and law-abiding, but they weren't saints. They were living in huts in the forest and cooking their food over

13

campfires while the villagers lived in manors and palaces, waited on by servants. So the cannibals moved into the villagers' houses. There were so many rooms in the houses that it took the villagers some time to notice, but when they finally did, they were angry.

"We never said you could live with us!" the villagers said. "You're dirty cannibals who eat human flesh! Go stay in the woods!"

"If you don't let us live in your houses," the cannibals replied, "we'll stop buying your limbs and go back to Meek. Then you won't be able to pay your loans and you'll lose everything."

The villagers didn't know what to do. They didn't want cannibals in their houses, but neither could they imagine going back to the way they used to live. In fact, things would be worse than before: not only would they be homeless, disfigured, and half blind, but they wouldn't even have swamps to farm because they'd filled them all in. It was unthinkable.

Grudgingly, they let the cannibals stay. The cannibals spread out among all the houses in the village (except Farmer Hayworth's—no one wanted to live in his crude wooden shack). They took the master suites and largest bedrooms and made the villagers move into their own guest rooms, *some of which did not even have en-suite bathrooms!* Mister Bachelard was forced to live in his chicken coop. Mister Anderson moved into his cellar. (It was very nice for a cellar, but still.)

The villagers complained incessantly about the new arrangement. (They still had tongues, after all.)

"Your cooking smells make me sick!" Mrs. Sally said to her cannibals.

"The tourists keep asking about you, and it's embarrassing!" Mister Pullman shouted at his cannibals, startling them as they read quietly in the study.

"If you don't move out, I'll tell the authorities you've been kid-napping children and cooking them into quiches!" Mister Bettelheim threatened.

"One doesn't cook a quiche, one *bakes* a quiche," replied his canni-bal, a cultivated Spaniard named Héctor.

"I don't care!" shouted Mister Bettelheim, going quite red in the face.

After some weeks of this, Héctor decided he couldn't take it any-more. He offered Mister Bettelheim every penny he had left on earth if he would just sell Héctor his tongue.

Mister Bettelheim did not reject the offer out of hand. He gave it careful thought and consideration. Without his tongue, he'd no longer be able to complain or make threats against Héctor. But with the money Héctor was promising, he could build a second house on his property and live *there*, away from Héctor, and he'd no longer have anything to complain about. And who else in the village would have not one but two golden-domed marble houses?

Now, if Mister Bettelheim had asked Farmer Hayworth's advice, his old friend would have told him not to take the cannibal's deal. *If the smell of Héctor's cooking bothers you, come and live with me,* Hayworth would have offered. *I have more than enough room in my house.* But Mister Bettelheim had shunned Farmer Hayworth, as had the rest of the village, so he didn't ask—and even if he had, Bettelheim was too proud, and would rather live without a tongue than in Hayworth's sad little house.

So Bettelheim went to Héctor and said, "Okay."

Héctor drew his carving knife, which was always sheathed at his side. "Yes?"

15

"Yes," Bettelheim said, and stuck out his tongue.

Héctor did the deed. He stuffed Bettelheim's mouth with cotton to stop the bleeding. He carried the tongue into the kitchen, fried it in truffle oil with a pinch of salt, and ate it. Then he took all the money he'd promised Bettelheim, gave it to Bettelheim's servants, and dismissed them. Limbless, tongueless, and very angry, Bettelheim grunted and wiggled around on the floor. Héctor picked him up, carried him outside, and tied him to a stake in a shady part of the back garden. He watered and fed Bettelheim twice a day, and like a fruiting vine Bettelheim grew limbs for Héctor to eat. Héctor felt a little bad about it, but not too bad. Eventually he married a nice cannibal girl and together they raised a cannibal family, all fed by the peculiar man in the back garden.

Such was the fate of all the villagers—all but Farmer Hayworth, who kept his limbs and lived in his little house and farmed his swamp like he always had. He didn't bother his new neighbors, and they didn't bother him. He had everything he needed, and so did they.

And they lived happily ever after.

The Fork-Tongued Princess

n the ancient kingdom of Frankenbourg there was a princess who had a peculiar secret: in her mouth hid a long, forked tongue and across her back lay shimmering, diamond-patterned scales. Because she had developed these serpentine characteristics during her teenage years and rarely opened her mouth for fear of being found out, she had been able to keep them secret from everyone but her handmaiden. Not even her father, the king, knew.

It was a lonely life for the princess, as she rarely spoke to anyone for fear they'd catch a glimpse of her forked tongue. But her real trouble was this: she was to be married to a prince from Galatia.[1] They'd never seen each other, but her beauty was so renowned that he'd agreed to the match anyway, and they were to meet for the first time on their wedding day, which was fast approaching. Their union would cement relations between Frankenbourg and Galatia, ensure prosperity for both regions,

---

1. The country names here are fictional, though in some regional versions of the tale they are substituted with real places. In one telling Frankenbourg is Spain, in another Galatia is Persia; the story, in any event, remains the same.

and create a pact of defense against their hated mutual enemy, the war-like principality of Frisia. The princess knew the marriage was politically necessary, but she was terrified the prince would reject her once he discovered her secret.

"Don't worry," counseled her handmaiden. "He'll see your beautiful face, come to know your beautiful heart, and forgive the rest."

"And if he doesn't?" the princess replied. "Our best hope for peace will be ruined, and I'll live the rest of my days a spinster!"

The kingdom prepared for a royal wedding. The palace was hung with golden silks, and chefs from across the land came to prepare a lavish feast. Finally, the prince arrived with his royal entourage. He climbed out of his carriage and greeted the king warmly.

"And where is my bride-to-be?" he asked.

He was shown into a reception hall where the princess was waiting.

"Princess!" cried the prince. "You're even lovelier than your reputation had me believe."

The princess smiled and bowed, but would not open her mouth to speak.

"What's the matter?" said the prince. "Have I struck you dumb with my good looks?"

The princess blushed and shook her head.

"Ah," the prince replied, "then you *don't* find me handsome, is that it?"

Alarmed, the princess shook her head again—that wasn't what she'd meant at all!—but she could see she was only making things worse.

"Say something, girl, this is no time to be tongue-tied!" hissed the king.

"Pardon me, sire," said the handmaiden, "but perhaps the princess would be more comfortable speaking with the prince for the first time in private."

The princess nodded gratefully.

"It isn't proper," the king grumbled, "but I suppose under the circumstances . . ."

His guards showed the prince and princess to a room where they could be alone.

"Well?" said the prince once the guards had gone. "What do you think of me?"

Covering her mouth with her hand, the princess said, "I think you're very handsome."

"Why do you hide your mouth when you speak?" the prince asked.

"It's my habit," the princess replied. "I'm sorry if you find it strange."

"You *are* strange. But I could learn to live with it, given your beauty!"

The princess's heart soared, but then crashed back to earth just as quickly. It would only be a matter of time before the prince discovered her secret. Though she could have waited until they married to reveal it, she knew it wasn't right to deceive him.

"I have something to confess," she said, still speaking with her mouth covered, "and I'm afraid that when you learn what it is, you won't want to marry me."

"Nonsense," said the prince. "What is it? Oh no—we're cousins, aren't we?"

"It isn't that," she said.

"Well," the prince said confidently, "there's nothing that could stop me wanting to marry you."

"I hope you're a man of your word," said the princess, and then she took away her hand and showed him her forked tongue.

"Stars above!" cried the prince, recoiling.

"That's not all," said the princess, and slipping one arm out of her dress, she showed him the scales that covered her back.

The prince was flabbergasted, then furious. "I could never marry a monster like you!" he cried. "I can't believe you and your father tried to trick me!"

"He didn't!" she said. "My father doesn't know anything about it!"

"Well, he's going to!" the prince fumed. "This is an outrage!"

He stormed out of the room to go tell the king, and the princess chased after, begging him not to.

It was just then that five Frisian assassins, who had disguised themselves as chefs, pulled daggers from their cakes and ran from the kitchens toward the king's room. The prince was just about to reveal the princess's secret when they broke down the door. While the assassins killed his guards, the cowardly king dove into a wardrobe and hid himself beneath a pile of clothes.

The assassins turned on the prince and princess.

"Don't kill me!" the prince cried. "I'm just an errand boy from another land!"

"Nice try," said the lead assassin. "You're the prince of Galatia, and you're here to marry the princess and form an alliance against us. Prepare to die!"

The prince ran to a window and tried to force it open, leaving the princess to face the assassins by herself. As they came toward her with their bloody daggers drawn, she felt a strange pressure building behind her tongue.

One after another they lunged at her. One after another, the princess launched streams of venomous poison into their faces, and all but one fell writhing to the ground and died. The fifth assassin fled from the room, terrified, and escaped.

The princess was as surprised as anyone. It was something she'd never known she could do; then again, she had never been threatened with death before. The prince, who was already halfway out the window, pulled himself back into the room and regarded both the dead assassins and the princess with amazement.

"*Now* will you marry me?" the princess said.

"Absolutely not," he replied, "but as a token of my gratitude, I won't tell your father why."

He grabbed a discarded dagger and rushed from assassin to assassin, stabbing their dead bodies.

"What are you doing?" said the bewildered princess.

The king emerged from his wardrobe. "Are they dead?" he said, his voice trembling.

"Yes, Your Majesty," said the prince, holding up the dagger. "I killed them all!"

The princess was shocked by his lie, but held her tongue.

"Magnificent!" cried the king. "You're the hero of Frankenbourg, my boy—and on your wedding day, no less!"

"Ah—about that," the prince said. "Regretfully, there will be no wedding."

"What!" shouted the king. "Why not?"

"I've just received word that the princess and I are cousins," said the prince. "Such a shame!"

And without so much as a backward glance, the prince slipped out of the room, gathered his entourage, and took off in his carriage.

"This is preposterous!" the king fumed. "That boy is no more my

23

daughter's cousin than I'm this chair's uncle. I won't allow my family to be treated this way!"

The king was so enraged that he threatened to go to war with Galatia. The princess knew she couldn't allow this to happen, and so one evening she requested an audience with her father alone and revealed the secret she'd been hiding so long. He called off his war plans, but he was so angry with his daughter, and so humiliated, that he locked her in the dankest cell of his dungeon.

"Not only are you a liar and a beast," he said, spitting through the bars of her cell, "you're not marriageable!"

He said it as if that were the greatest sin of all.

"But, Father," said the princess, "I'm still your daughter, aren't I?"

"Not anymore," the king replied, and turned his back on her.

The princess knew she could use her acidic venom to burn through the lock of her cell door and escape, but instead she waited, hoping her father might come to his senses and forgive her.[2] For months she subsisted on gruel and shivered through the nights on a stone slab, but her father did not come. The princess's only visitor was her handmaiden.

One day, the handmaiden arrived with news.

"Has my father forgiven me?" the princess asked eagerly.

"I'm afraid not," the handmaiden replied. "He's told the kingdom you're dead. Your funeral is tomorrow."

The princess was heartbroken. She broke out of the dungeon that

2. There used to be a highly acidic liquid you could buy on the peculiar black market. The bottles were wrapped in snakeskin, and the stuff inside could burn through metal. It was called Princess Spit—in honor, no doubt, of this tale. After a number of unfortunate incidents involving its misuse, peculiar authorities shut down its manufacture. These days, bottles of Princess Spit are rare collectors' items.

very night, escaped the palace, and with her handmaiden she left the kingdom and her old life behind. They traveled incognito for months, wandering the land, taking domestic work where they could find it. The princess smeared her face with dirt so she would not be recognized and never opened her mouth to anyone but the handmaiden, who told people that the dirty-faced girl she traveled with was mute.

Then one day they heard a story about a prince in the faraway kingdom of Thrace whose body sometimes assumed a form so peculiar that it had become a national scandal.

"Could it possibly be true?" said the princess. "Could he be like me?"

"I say it's worth finding out," the handmaiden replied.

So they set out on a long journey. It took two weeks to cross the Pitiless Waste on horseback, and two weeks more to cross the Great Cataract by ship. When they finally arrived in the kingdom of Thrace they were sunburned, windburned, and nearly broke.

"I couldn't possibly meet the prince looking like this!" the princess said, so they spent the last of the money they'd earned and went to a bathhouse, where they were washed and perfumed and anointed with oils. When they emerged, the princess looked so beautiful that she turned the heads of everyone who saw her, male or female.

"I'll show my father I'm marriageable!" the princess said. "Let's go meet this peculiar prince."

So they went to the palace and asked for him, but the answer they got was disappointing indeed.

"I'm sorry," a palace guard told them, "but the prince is dead."

"What happened?" asked the handmaiden.

"He fell ill with a mysterious disease and died in the night," said the guard. "It was all very sudden."

"That's exactly what the king said happened to you," the handmaiden whispered to the princess.

That night they snuck into the palace dungeon, and in the darkest, dankest cell, they found a giant garden slug with the head of a rather handsome young man.

"Are you the prince?" the handmaiden asked him.

"I am," the repulsive thing answered. "When I'm feeling dejected, my body turns into a gelatinous, quivering mass. My mother finally found out and locked me down here, and now, as you can see, I've become a slug almost head to toe." The prince wriggled toward the bars of his cell, his body leaving a dark stain on the floor behind him. "I'm sure she'll come to her senses any day now, though, and let me out."

The princess and the handmaiden exchanged an awkward glance.

"Well, I have good news and bad news," said the handmaiden. "The bad news is your mother's told everyone you're dead."

The prince began to wail and moan, and immediately a pair of gelatinous antennae began to grow from his forehead. Now even his head was turning slug.

"Wait!" the handmaiden said. "There's still the good news!"

"Oh yes, I forgot," the prince sniffled, and the antennae stopped growing. "What is it?"

"This is the princess of Frankenbourg," said the handmaiden.

The princess stepped forward into a pool of light, and for the first time the prince saw her fantastic beauty.

"You're a *princess*?" the prince stuttered, his eyes going wide.

"That's right," said the handmaiden. "And she's here to rescue you."

The prince was thrilled. "I don't believe it!" he said. "How?"

26

His antennae were shrinking back into his head and the tubelike mass of his upper body was already beginning to separate into arms and a torso. Just like that, he was turning human again.

"Like this!" said the princess, and she spat a stream of venomous acid into the lock of the prince's cell door. It began to hiss and smoke as the lock melted.

The prince recoiled in alarm. "What *are* you?" he said.

"I'm peculiar, like you!" the princess replied. "When my father found out my secret, he disowned me and locked me up, too. I know just how you're feeling!"

As she spoke, her forked tongue flicked from her mouth.

"And your tongue," the prince said. "That's part of what's . . . *wrong* with you?"

"And this," the princess said, and she slipped an arm from her dress and showed him the scales across her back.

"I see," said the prince, his voice sorrowful again. "I should've known this was too good to be true."

As a tear rolled down his cheek, his arms began to disappear, joining again with his torso in a wobbly mass of slug flesh.

"Why are you sad?" the princess said. "We're a perfect match! Together we could show our parents that we're not unmarriageable, and we're not trash. We can unite our kingdoms, and one day, perhaps, take our rightful place on the throne!"

"You must be mad!" the prince shouted. "How could I ever love you? You're a disgusting freak!"

The princess was speechless. She couldn't believe what he was saying.

"Oh, this is so humiliating!" the slug prince bawled, and then

27

antennae sprung from his forehead, his face disappeared, and he became a slug from head to toe, quivering and moaning as he struggled to cry without a mouth.

The princess and the handmaiden turned away, stomachs heaving, and left the ungrateful prince to rot in his dungeon.

"I believe I'm done with princes forever," the princess said, "peculiar or otherwise."

They crossed the Great Cataract and the Pitiless Waste once again, and returned to Frankenbourg to find it at war with both Galatia and Frisia, which had united against it. The king had been overthrown and jailed, and the Frisians had installed a duke to govern Frankenbourg. The duke was a bachelor, and once his rule had been established and the country pacified, he began searching for a bride. The duke's emissary discovered the princess working in an inn.

"You there!" he shouted, calling her away from a table she was cleaning. "The duke is looking for a bride."

"Good luck to him," she replied. "I'm not interested."

"Your opinion doesn't matter," the emissary replied. "Come with me at once."

"But I'm not royal!" she lied.

"That doesn't matter, either. The duke merely wants to find the most beautiful woman in the kingdom, and that may well be you."

The princess was beginning to regard her beauty as something of a curse.

She was given a nice dress to wear and brought before the duke. When she saw his face, a cold chill spread through her. This Frisian duke had been one of the assassins who had come to kill her; he was the lone assassin who had fled.

"Do I know you from somewhere?" the duke said. "You look familiar."

The princess was tired of hiding and tired of lying, so she told the truth. "You tried to kill me once, and my father. I was once the princess of Frankenbourg."

"I thought you were dead!" said the duke.

"No," she replied, "that was a lie my father made up."

"Then I'm not the only one who tried to kill you," he said, and smiled.

"I suppose not."

"I like your honesty," said the duke, "as well as your fortitude. You're made of strong stuff, and we Frisians admire that. I can't make you my wife because you might murder me in my sleep, but if you'll accept the position, I'd like to appoint you as my adviser. Your unique perspective would be valuable indeed."

The princess happily accepted. She moved back into the palace with her handmaiden, took a position of prominence in the duke's government, and never again covered her mouth when she spoke, as she no longer had to hide who she was.

After some time had passed, she paid her father a visit in the dungeons. He was wearing grimy sackcloth and not looking very kingly at all.

"Get out of here," he growled at her. "You're a traitor and I have nothing to say to you."

"Well, I have something to say to you," the princess replied. "Though I'm still angry at you, I want you to know you are forgiven. I understand now that what you did to me wasn't the action of an evil man, but a common one."

29

"Fine, thank you for the wonderful speech," said the king. "Now go away."

"As you wish," said the princess. She started to go, then stopped at the doorway. "By the way, they're planning to hang you in the morning."

At this news the king curled into a ball and began to snivel and cry. It was such a pathetic sight that the princess was moved to pity. Despite all her father had done, she felt her bitterness toward him melting away. She used her venom to melt the lock from his cell, secreted him out of the jailhouse, disguised him as a beggar, and sent him running in the same direction she had once fled the kingdom. He did not thank her, nor even look back at her. And then he was gone, and she was gripped by a sudden, wild happiness—for her act of kindness had freed them both.

The First Ymbryne

———◆———

Editor's note:

While we can be certain that many of the Tales' *characters really
lived and walked the earth, it can be difficult to confirm much of their
factualness beyond that. In the centuries before our stories were
written down, they were disseminated as oral tradition, and thus
highly subject to change, each teller embellishing the tales as she saw
fit. The result is that today they are more legend than history, and their
value—beyond simply being compelling stories—is primarily as moral
lessons. The story of Britain's first ymbryne, however, is a notable
exception. It is one of the few tales whose historical authenticity can be
thoroughly accounted for, the events it describes having been verified
not only by many contemporaneous sources, but by the ymbryne herself
(in her famous book of encyclical addresses,* A Gathering of Tail
Feathers*). That is why I consider it the most significant of the* Tales,
*it being equally a moral parable, a ripping good yarn, and an
important chronicle of peculiar history.*

—MN

he first ymbryne wasn't a woman who could turn herself into a bird, but a bird who could turn herself into a woman. She was born into a family of goshawks, fierce hunters who didn't appreciate their sister's habit of becoming a fleshy, earthbound creature at unpredictable times, her sudden changes in size toppling them out of their nest, and her odd, babbling speech spoiling their hunts. Her father gave her the name Ymeene, which in the shrill language of goshawks meant "strange one," and she felt the lonely burden of that strangeness from the time she was old enough to hold up her head.

Goshawks are territorial and proud, and love nothing more than a good, bloody fight. Ymeene was no different, and when a turf war erupted between their family and a band of harriers, she fought bravely, determined to prove she was every bit the goshawk her brothers were. They were outnumbered by the larger, stronger birds, but even when his children began to die in the skirmishes, Ymeene's father would not admit defeat. In the end they repelled the harriers, but Ymeene was wounded and all her siblings but one were killed. Wondering what it had all been for, she asked her father why they had not simply run away and found another nest to live in.

"We had to defend the honor of our family," he told her.

"But now our family is gone," Ymeene replied. "Where's the honor in that?"

"I don't suppose a creature like you would understand," he said, and straightening his feathers he leaped into the air and flew away to go hunting.

Ymeene did not join him. She had lost her taste for the hunt, and for blood and fighting, too, which for a goshawk was even stranger than turning into a human now and then. Perhaps she was never meant to be a hawk, she thought, as she winged down to the forest floor and landed on human legs. Perhaps she was born in the wrong body.

Ymeene wandered for a long time. She lingered around human settlements, studying them from the safety of treetops. Because she had stopped hunting, it was hunger that gave her the nerve to finally walk into a village and sneak bites of their food—roasted corn put out for chickens, pies left to cool on windowsills, unwatched pots of soup—and she found she had a taste for it. She learned some human language so that she could talk to them, and discovered that she enjoyed their company even more than their food. She liked the way they laughed and sang and showed one another love. So she chose a village at random and went to live there.

A kindly old man let her stay in his barn, and his wife taught Ymeene to sew so she would have a trade. Everything was going swimmingly until, a few days after she'd arrived, the village baker saw her turn into a bird. She hadn't yet grown accustomed to sleeping in human form, so every night she changed into a goshawk, flew up into the trees, and fell asleep with her head tucked under her wing. The shocked villagers accused her of witchcraft and chased her away with torches.

Disappointed but undeterred, Ymeene went wandering again and found another village in which to settle. This time she was careful not to let anyone see her change into a bird, but the villagers seemed to distrust her regardless. To most people Ymeene had a strange way about her—she had been raised by hawks, after all—and it wasn't long before she was chased from this new village, too. She grew sad, and wondered if there was any place in the world she truly belonged.

One morning, on the verge of despair, she lay watching the sun rise in a forest glade. It was a spectacle of such transcendent beauty that it made her forget her troubles for a moment, and when it was over, she wished desperately to see it once more. In an instant the sky went dark and the dawn broke all over again, and she suddenly realized she had a talent other than her ability to change form: she could make small moments repeat themselves. She amused herself with this trick for days, repeating the leap of a graceful deer or a fleeting slant of afternoon sun just so she could better appreciate their beauty, and it cheered her up immensely. She was repeating the first fall of virgin snow when a voice startled her.

"Excuse me," he said, "but are *you* making that happen?"

She spun around to see a young man wearing a short green tunic and shoes made from fish skin. It was an odd outfit, but stranger still was that he carried his head under the crook of his arm, disconnected entirely from his neck.

"Excuse *me*," she replied, "but what's happened to your head?"

"Frightfully sorry!" he said, reacting as if he'd just realized his pants were unbuttoned, and, with great embarrassment, he popped his head back onto his neck. "How rude of me."

He said his name was Englebert, and as she had nowhere else to

36

go, he invited her back to his camp. It was a ragged settlement of tents and open cook fires, and the few dozen people who lived there were every bit as strange as Englebert. They were so strange, in fact, that most of them had been chased out of other villages—just like Ymeene. They welcomed her even after she showed them how she could turn herself into a hawk, and in turn they showed her some of the unusual talents they possessed. It seemed she was not alone in the world. Perhaps, she thought, there was a place for her after all.

These were, of course, the early peculiars of Britain, and what Ymeene didn't realize was that she had joined them during one of the darkest periods in their history. There had been a time when peculiars were accepted—even revered—by normal people, with whom they mixed easily. But an age of ignorance had dawned of late, and normals had grown suspicious of them. Whenever something tragic happened that couldn't be explained by the rudimentary science of the day, peculiars were made the scapegoats. When the village of Little Disappointment woke one morning to find all their sheep burned to a crisp, did the villagers realize that a lightning storm had killed them? No, they blamed the local peculiar and drove him into the wilderness. When the seamstresses of Stitch didn't stop laughing for an entire week, did the villagers blame the wool they had just imported, which was infested with mites that carried Laughing Flu? Of course not: they pinned it on a pair of peculiar sisters and hanged them.

Such outrages were repeated across the land, driving peculiars out of normal society and into bands like the one Ymeene had joined. It was no utopia; they lived together because they could trust no one else. Their village leader was a peculiar named Tombs, a red-bearded giant cursed with the squeaky voice of a sparrow. His tenor made it difficult for others to take him seriously, but he took himself *quite* seriously, and never let anyone forget that he sat on the Council of Important Peculiars.[1]

Ymeene avoided Tombs, having developed something of an allergy to prideful men, and instead spent her days with her funny, occasionally headless friend, Englebert. She helped him till the camp's vegetable patch and collect wood for cook fires, and he helped her get to know the other peculiars. They took to Ymeene instantly, and she began to think of the camp as her adopted home and the peculiars as her second family. She told them about life as a hawk and amused them with her trick of repeating things—once looping a moment where Tombs tripped over a sleeping dog until the whole village hurt from laughing—and they regaled her with tales of peculiardom's colorful history. There was, for a while, peace. It was the happiest time Ymeene could remember.

Every few days, though, the village's tranquil bubble was punctured by woeful tidings from the outside world. Desperate peculiars arrived in a steady stream, seeking refuge from terror and persecution. Each had a familiar tale to tell: they had lived peacefully among normals their whole lives, until one day they were accused of some absurd crime and chased out, lucky to escape with their lives. (Like the unfortunate sisters of Stitch, not all were so lucky.) The peculiars welcomed the new arrivals just as they had welcome Ymeene, but after nearly a month of influx the

38

---

1. The Council of Important Peculiars, made up entirely of men, predated the Council of Ymbrynes by a great many years. It was composed of a dozen chummy councilmen who met twice a year to write and amend the laws peculiars were supposed to follow, which mainly concerned conflict resolution (duels were permitted), the circumstances under which peculiars were allowed to use their abilities around normals (whenever it suited them), and the myriad penalties for breaking the rules (ranging from tongue-lashings to banishment).

village swelled from fifteen peculiars to fifty. There wasn't enough space or food for things to continue this way indefinitely, and a sense of foreboding began to weigh heavily upon the peculiars.

One day another representative from the Council of Important Peculiars arrived. He wore a grim expression and disappeared into Tombs's tent for hours, and when he and Tombs finally emerged, they gathered everyone together to deliver some distressing news. The normals had already driven peculiars out of many of their towns and villages, and now they had decided to drive them out of Oddfordshire altogether. They had assembled a force of armed fighters that would soon be on the peculiars' doorstep. The question now was whether to fight or flee.

Needless to say, the peculiars were alarmed, and not a little hesitant.

A young woman looked around them and said, "This hill and these flimsy tents aren't worth dying for. Why don't we pack our things and go hide in the woods?"

"I don't know about all of you," said Tombs, "but I'm tired of running. I say we stand and fight. We must reclaim our dignity!"

"That is also the council's official recommendation," added the grim-faced councilman, nodding.

"But we aren't soldiers," said Englebert. "We don't know the first thing about fighting."

"They're a small force, and lightly armed," said Tombs. "They think we're cowards who will flee at the first sign of force. But they underestimate us."

"But won't we need weapons?" asked another man. "Swords and clubs?"

"You surprise me, Eustace," Tombs replied. "Can't you turn a man's face inside out just by pulling his nose?"

"Well, yes," the man said sheepishly.

"And, Millicent Neary, I've seen you light fires with only your breath. Imagine how terrified those normals will be when you set their clothes ablaze!"

"You paint quite a picture!" said Millicent. "Yes, it would be something to send *them* running for a change."

At that, the crowd began to mutter.

"Yes, it *would* be something."

"Those normals have had it coming for a long time."

"Did you hear what they did to Titus Smith? Cut him into bits and fed him to his own pigs!"

"If we don't stand up for ourselves now, they'll never stop."

"Justice for Titus! Justice for us all!"

With little effort, the councilmen had whipped the peculiars into a fervor. Even mild-mannered Englebert was spoiling for a fight. Ymeene, whose stomach had turned at the first mention of a battle, couldn't listen anymore. She slunk out of the village and went for a long walk in the woods. Returning at dusk, she found Englebert by his cook fire. His temper had cooled, but his resolve to fight had not.

"Come away with me," Ymeene said to him. "We'll start over somewhere else."

"Where will we go?" he replied. "They want to chase us out of Oddfordshire!"

"Wontshire. Therefordshire. Peacewickshire. You'd rather die in Oddfordshire than live elsewhere?"

"They're just a few dozen men," said Englebert. "How would it look if we ran away from such a puny threat?"

Even with victory practically assured, Ymeene wanted no part of it.

"How it looks isn't worth sacrificing a single hair from our heads, much less a life."

"So you won't fight?"

"I lost one family to war already. I won't watch another throw itself willingly into the furnace."

"If you leave, they'll think you a traitor," said Englebert. "You'll never be able to come back."

She looked at him. "What will you think?"

Englebert stared into the fire, struggling for words. The silence between them seemed answer enough, so Ymeene slipped away and walked to her tent. As she lay down to sleep, a great sadness stole over her. She was sure it would be her last night as a human.

Ymeene left at the first inkling of dawn, before anyone else had woken. She couldn't bear to say good-bye. She walked to the edge of the camp and turned into a hawk, and as she leaped into the air, she wondered if she would ever find another group that would accept her, human or avian.

Ymeene had only been flying a few minutes when she spotted the normals' fighting force massed below. But it was no loose brigade of a few dozen men—it was an army of hundreds, and they blanketed the hills in glinting armor.

The peculiars would be slaughtered! She turned around at once and flew back to warn them. She found Tombs in his tent and told them what she'd seen.

He didn't seem surprised in the least.

He had *known*.

"Why didn't you tell them so many soldiers were coming?" Ymeene said. "You lied!"

41

"They would have been terrified," he said. "They would not have comported themselves with dignity."

"They *should* be terrified!" she shouted. "They should have fled by now!"

"It wouldn't have done any good," he said. "The normals' king has ordered Britain cleansed of peculiars from mountains to sea. They would find us eventually."

"Not if we leave Britain," Ymeene said.

"Leave Britain!" he said, shocked. "But we've been here hundreds of years!"

"And we'll be dead a lot longer than that," Ymeene replied.

"It's a matter of honor," Tombs said. "I suppose a bird wouldn't understand."

"I understand all too well," she replied, and went out to warn the others.

But it was too late: the normals' army was on their doorstep, a swarm of well-armed soldiers already visible in the distance. Worse yet, the peculiars couldn't even run—the normals were closing in from all sides.

The peculiars huddled in their camp, terrified. Death seemed inevitable. Ymeene could easily have changed form and flown to safety— the peculiars urged her to, in fact—but she could not bring herself to leave. They had been tricked, lied to, and the sacrifice they were about to make was no longer voluntary. To leave now would not have felt like an exercise of her principles, but like abandonment and treachery. So she walked through the camp, embracing her friends. Englebert hugged her the hardest, and even after he'd let go, he spent a long moment gazing at her.

"What are you doing?" she asked him.

"Memorizing the face of my friend," he said. "So that I might recall it even in death."

Silence fell over them and over the camp, and for a while the only sounds were the thunder and clang of the approaching army. And then the sun came out suddenly from behind a dark cloud, bathing the land in glinting light, and Ymeene thought the sight so beautiful that she wished she could see it once more before they were killed. So she repeated it, and the peculiars were so mesmerized that she repeated it a second time. Only then did they notice that, in the minutes they had spent watching the sun, the normals' army had not come any closer. With every repetition, their enemies faded and reappeared farther away, many hundreds of yards in the distance.

It was then that Ymeene realized her time-looping talent had a use she'd never fully understood—one that would change peculiar society forever, though she couldn't have known it then. She'd made a safe place for them, a bubble of stalled time, and the peculiars watched in fascination as the normals' army advanced toward them and then faded away, over and over again, in a three-minute loop.

43

"How long can you keep this going?" Englebert asked her.

"I don't know," she admitted. "I've never repeated something more than a few times. But for quite a while, I think."

Tombs burst out of his tent, baffled and angry. "What are you doing?" he shouted at Ymeene. "Stop that!"

"Why should I?" she said. "I'm saving all our lives!"

"You're only delaying the inevitable," Tombs replied. "I order you, by authority of the council, to desist immediately!"

"A pox on your council!" said Millicent Neary. "You're nothing but liars!"

Tombs had begun to enumerate the punishments that awaited anyone who defied the council's orders when Eustace Corncrake marched up to him and pulled his nose, which caused Tombs's face to turn inside out. He ran away yelping and threatening recriminations, his head all pink and soft.

Ymeene kept looping. The peculiars rallied around her, cheering her on, but worrying quietly that she would not be able to keep it going forever. Ymeene shared their concern: she had to repeat the loop every three minutes, so she could not sleep—but eventually her body would force her to, and the army that loomed perpetually in the distance would close in and finally crush them.

After two days and a night, Ymeene could no longer trust herself to stay awake, so Englebert volunteered to sit beside her, and every time her eyes fell closed he would nudge her. After three days and two nights, when Englebert began to fall asleep himself, Eustace Corncrake volunteered to sit by his side and nudge *him*, and then, when Eustace began to lose his battle with sleep, Millicent Neary volunteered to sit by him and drip water on his face whenever his eyes closed—so that eventually the whole camp of peculiars were sitting in a long chain, helping one another to help Englebert to help Ymeene stay awake.

After four days and three nights, Ymeene still had not missed a loop reset. She had, however, begun to hallucinate from exhaustion. She thought her lost brothers had come to see her, five goshawks flying loops of their own above the camp. They screeched words at her that made no sense:

Again!

Another!

Again! Again!

Loop-the-loop to double its skin!

She squeezed her eyes shut and shook her head, then drank some of the water Millicent Neary was dripping on Eustace Corncrake. When she looked up again her ghostly brothers were gone, but their words stayed with her. She wondered if her brothers—or some part of her own, embedded instinct—were trying to tell her something useful.

Again, again.

The answer came to her on the fifth day. Or rather *an* answer: she wasn't sure if it was the right one, but she was entirely certain that she wouldn't last another day. Before long, no amount of nudging would keep her from sleep.

So: she reset the loop. (She'd long since lost count of how many times she'd made that sun peek out from behind that cloud, but it had to be thousands.) And then, just a few seconds after having looped the loop, she made another one—*inside* the first loop.

The results were instantaneous and bizarre. There was a strange sort of doubling of everything around them—the sun, the cloud, the army in the distance—as if her vision had blurred. The world took a short while to come back into focus, and when it did, it was all a bit *older* than before. The sun was farther behind the cloud. The army was farther away. And this time it took six minutes, not three, for the sun to come out from behind the cloud.

So she looped the loop twice a second time, and then their loop was twelve minutes, and she did it a third time and it was twenty-four. And when she'd gotten it up to an hour, she took a nap. And then she looped the loop again and again, and it was like she was filling a vessel with air or water, she could feel its skin expanding to hold all this new time, until it was as tight as a drum and she knew it would hold no more.

45

The loop Ymeene had made was now twenty-four hours long, and it began the previous morning, long before there was an army on the horizon. Her fellow peculiars were so impressed and so grateful that they tried to call her Queen Ymeene and Your Majesty, but she wouldn't let them. She was just Ymeene, and it was the greatest joy she'd known to have made a safe place—a nest—for her friends.

Though they were safe from the normals' aggression, their problems were far from over. The army that had nearly destroyed them went on to terrorize peculiars across the land, and as word spread of a time loop in Oddfordshire, survivors and refugees arrived with increasing frequency.[2]

In a few weeks their number grew from fifty to twice that. Among them were several members of the Council of Important Peculiars (including Tombs, whose face had flipped right side out again). While they no longer seemed interested in shutting down the loop, the councilmen tried to assert their authority by insisting that no new arrivals be admitted. But everyone deferred to Ymeene—it was her loop, after all—and she wouldn't hear of turning people away, even though the camp was bursting.

The councilmen grew angry and threatened everyone with punishment. The people grew angry, too, and accused the council of lying

2. While this tale doesn't mention them, likely because they are too numerous to mention, many remarkable discoveries were made at this time regarding the behavior and function of loops. These included the concept of arrested aging, the limits of accessibility for non-peculiars, a loop's dual exits into past and present, and perhaps even the rudiments of time-stream theory and the problems of parallel streams. All of which makes Ymeene not only Britain's first ymbryne but a true pioneer in loopology. Neither should the contributions of her friend Englebert be overlooked: within his removable head dwelled a keen scientific mind, and if not for his detailed notes, many of Ymeene's breakthroughs would have been lost.

to trick them into going to war. The councilmen pointed their fingers at Tombs, claiming he had acted alone—though this was obviously not true—and that his deception had not been sanctioned by the other councilmen. They further pointed their fingers at Ymeene and accused her of usurping their rightful authority, an offense punishable by banishment to the Pitiless Waste. At which point the people rose up in her defense, threw mud (and possibly a bit of excrement) at the councilmen, and drove them out of the loop.[3]

In the weeks that followed, the peculiars looked to Ymeene for leadership. In addition to making sure the loop kept looping, she was called upon to resolve personal disputes, to cast deciding votes about which of the council's many rules should be retained and which jettisoned, to punish breakers of what rules they kept, and so on. She adapted quickly to her new role, but was baffled by it, too. Of all the peculiars in the loop, she was the newest and the least experienced. She'd only been a full-time human for six months! But her comrades viewed her inexperience as a boon: she was fresh and unbiased, neutral and fair, and had about her a quiet, dignified wisdom that seemed more of the avian world than the human.

But for all her wisdom, Ymeene still could not solve their biggest problem: how more than one hundred peculiars could live in a space that was only three hundred feet from end to end. Once established, a loop can be made to hold more time, but not more space—and Ymeene had only enlooped their small camp's few dozen tents. They hadn't

---

3. This small, popular revolt was the beginning of matriarchal ymbryne leadership in peculiardom, but it was not a clean break. The council and its cronies did not let go of power easily, and in years following they staged a series of unsuccessful coups. But that's a story for another time.

much food, and though their stores reappeared each day with the cy-cling of the loop, it was never enough to feed all of them. (Outside their loop a hard winter had set in, so there was little to be hunted or foraged; they were more likely to find a roving gang of normals than a meal, for the normals had become obsessed with finding the peculiars who had disappeared right in front of their eyes.)

Ymeene was talking it over with Englebert one night as they sat around a crowded cook fire.

"What are we to do?" she said. "If we stay here we'll starve, and if we leave we'll be hunted down."

Englebert had removed his head and placed it in his lap so that he could scratch the top of it with both hands, something he did when he was deep in thought. "Could you make a larger loop someplace with plen-tiful food?" he asked. "If we're careful not to be seen, we could all move."

"When the weather thaws, perhaps. We'd likely freeze to death in any new loop I made now."

"Then we'll wait," he said. "We'll just have to starve a little, until a good thaw comes."

"And then what?" she said. "More peculiars in need will come, and soon we'll outgrow that loop, too. A limit will be reached. I can only handle so much responsibility."

Englebert sighed and scratched his head. "If only you could copy yourself."

A strange look came over Ymeene's face. "What was that you said?"

"If you could copy yourself," Englebert repeated. "Then you could make multiple loops, and we could spread out a bit. I worry about put-ting so many of us in one place. Factions will divide us and fights will break out. And if, Heaven forfend, something tragic were to happen to this loop, the population of peculiars in Britain would be halved in a single stroke."

Ymeene was facing Englebert, but her eyes were staring past him.

"What is it?" he said. "*Have* you thought of a way to copy yourself?"

"Perhaps," she replied. "Perhaps."

The next morning Ymeene gathered the peculiars and told them she was going away for a while. Ripples of panic spread through the crowd, though she assured them she'd be back in time to reset the loop. They begged her not to go, but she insisted it was crucial to their survival.

She left Englebert in charge, assumed bird form, and flew out of her loop for the first time since its creation. Soaring over the frozen forests of Oddfordshire, she asked the same question of every bird she saw: "Do you know any birds who can turn into humans?" She searched all day and night, but everywhere she went the answer was no. She returned to her loop late that night, tired and discouraged—but not defeated. She reset the loop, dodged Englebert's questions, and flew out again without a moment's rest.

She searched and searched until her wings and her eyes ached, thinking: "I couldn't really be the only creature in the world like me, could I?"

After another long day of fruitless scouting, she was almost convinced that she was absolutely unique. It was a thought that made her desperate—and desperately lonely.

Then, just as the sun was setting, and she was about to turn back toward her loop, Ymeene flew over a forest clearing and spied below her a flock of kestrels and among them, a young woman. It all happened in a flash. The kestrels saw her and took off, scattering into the woods. In the tumult, the young woman seemed to have disappeared. But where could she have gone so quickly?

Could she have turned into a kestrel and flown away with the others?

Ymeene dove after them and gave chase, and for an hour tried to track the kestrels down—but kestrels are the natural prey of goshawks, and they were terrified of Ymeene. She would have to try another approach.

It was dark. She returned to her loop, reset it, wolfed down five ears of roasted corn and two bowls of leek soup—flying all day was hungry work—and returned to the kestrels' woods the next morning. This time she approached their clearing not from the air as a goshawk, but on foot as a human. When the kestrels saw her they flew up into the trees and sat watching her, cautious but unafraid. Ymeene stood in the middle of the clearing and addressed them not in human language, or in go-talk (the speech of goshawks), but in the few halting words of kestrel she knew, as well as her human throat could reproduce them.

"One among you is not like the others," she said, "and it is to that young woman that I address myself. You are both bird and human. I am afflicted and blessed with the same ability, and I would very much like to speak with you."

The spectacle of a human speaking kestrel incited a flurry of chittering in the trees, and then Ymeene heard a flap of wings. After a few moments, a young woman showed herself from behind a tree trunk. She had dark, smooth skin and close-cropped hair, a tall, finely boned frame that was distinctly birdlike, and she wore furs and leathers to protect against the cold.

"Can you understand me?" Ymeene asked her in English.

The young woman gave a tentative nod. *A little*, she seemed to say.

"Can you speak human?" said Ymeene.

"*Sí, un poco,*" replied the young woman.

Ymeene recognized the language as human but couldn't understand the words. Perhaps the young woman was from a migratory clan, and had picked them up elsewhere.

"My name is Ymeene," she said, indicating herself. "What's yours?"

The young woman cleared her throat and made a loud cry in kestrel-ese.

"Perhaps we'll just call you Miss Kestrel for now," said Ymeene. "Miss Kestrel, I've an important question for you. Have you ever made something happen . . . *more than once?*"

She drew a large circle in the air with her finger, hoping the young woman would understand.

Miss Kestrel came forward a few paces, her eyes widening. Just then a clump of snow fell from a tree branch, and with a flourish of her arms, Miss Kestrel made it disappear from the ground and fall from the tree a second time.

"Yes!" Ymeene cried. "You can do it, too!" And then she waved her arm and repeated the snowfall, too, and Miss Kestrel's jaw fell open with astonishment.

They ran to each other, laughing, and clasped hands and shouted and then hugged, each chattering excitedly in a language the other could hardly understand. The kestrels in the trees were jubilant, too, and sensing that Ymeene was a friend, they flew down from their branches and fluttered around the two women, twittering with excitement.

The relief Ymeene felt was indescribable. Though she was peculiar even among peculiars, now she knew she was not alone. There were

51

more like her, which meant that—perhaps—peculiar society could be made a safer, saner place, no longer ruled by the shortsighted whims of prideful men. She had only an inkling of what form that society might take, but she knew that finding Miss Kestrel had been an important breakthrough. They spoke, in their halting way, for nearly an hour, and by the end of it Miss Kestrel had agreed to follow Ymeene back to the loop.

The rest, as they say, is history. Miss Kestrel came to live with the peculiars. Ymeene taught her everything she knew about loops, and soon Miss Kestrel was skilled enough to keep their loop going by herself. This allowed Ymeene to embark on long-distance expeditions to find more time-looping birdwomen like themselves—which she did, bringing their number to five—and when the new arrivals had been trained, and the hard, hungry winter had thawed into spring, they divided the peculiars among them and set out across the land to establish five new, permanent loops.

They were regarded as safe havens of sanity and order, and word of them spread quickly. Peculiars who had survived the purges traveled from all across Britain to seek refuge in them, though in order to be admitted they had to agree to live under the rules of the birdwomen. The women became known as *ymeenes*, to honor the first of their kind (though with the passage of time and the gradual shifting of tongues in Britain the word became *ymbryne*).

The ymbrynes held council twice a year to trade wisdom and collaborate. For many years Ymeene herself oversaw the proceedings, watching with pride as their network of ymbrynes and loops increased, and the number of peculiars they were able to protect grew to many hundreds. She lived to the ripe and happy age of one hundred and fifty-seven. For all those years she and Englebert shared a house (but never a room), for they loved each other in a steady, companionable way. It was the Black Plague, on one of its pitiless sweeps through Europe, that finally took her. When she was gone, all the peculiars she had saved who were still living, and all their children and grandchildren, risked their lives to cross hostile territory and carry her in a grand procession to the forest and, to the best of Englebert's reckoning, to the very tree in which she had been born, and they buried her there among its roots.[4]

---

4. Ymeene's tree was a destination for peculiar pilgrims for many years, but its location has long been lost. One of her tan and black tail feathers was saved, however, an ancient relic that can still be viewed in the Pantheon of Notables, safely behind glass.

The Woman
Who Befriended Ghosts

---•◦•---

here was once a peculiar woman named Hildy. She had a high laughing voice and dark brown skin, and she could see ghosts. She wasn't frightened by them at all. Her twin sister drowned when they were children, and when Hildy was growing up, her sister's ghost was her closest friend. They did everything together: ran through the poppy fields that surrounded their house, played stick-a-whack on the village green, and stayed up late telling each other scary stories about living people. The ghost of Hildy's sister even came to school with her. She would entertain Hildy by making rude faces at the teacher that no one else could see, and help her on examinations by looking at other students' answers and whispering them into Hildy's ear. (She could have shouted them and no one but Hildy would have heard, but it seemed prudent to whisper, just in case.)

On Hildy's eighteenth birthday, her sister got called away on ghost business.

"When will you be back?" Hildy asked, distraught. They hadn't been apart a single day since her sister died.

"Not for years," replied her sister. "I'll miss you terribly."

"Not more than I'll miss you," Hildy said miserably.

Hildy's sister hugged her, ghostly tears standing in her eyes. "Try to make some friends," she said, then vanished.

Hildy tried to take her sister's advice, but she had never had a living friend. She accepted an invitation to a party but couldn't bring herself to speak to anyone. Her father arranged a tea for Hildy with the daughter of a coworker, but Hildy was stiff and awkward, and the only thing she could think of to say was, "Have you ever played stick-a-whack?"

"That's a game for children," the woman replied, then made an excuse to leave early.

Hildy found she preferred the company of ghosts to living people, and so she decided to make some ghost friends. The trouble was how to do it. Even though Hildy could see ghosts, they were not easy to talk to. Ghosts, you see, are a bit like cats—they're never around when you want them, and rarely come when called.[1]

Hildy went to a cemetery. She stood around waiting for hours, but no ghosts came to talk to her. They watched Hildy from across the grass, standoffish and suspicious. She thought perhaps they'd been dead too long and had learned not to trust living people. Hoping the recently deceased would be easier to befriend, she started going to funerals. Because people she knew didn't die very often, she had to go to strangers' funerals. When the mourners would ask why she was there, Hildy would lie and say she was a distant relative, then ask whether the deceased had been a nice person, and had they enjoyed running in fields or playing

---

1. This is also true of grimbears, unless you have a special bond with one.

stick-a-whack? The mourners thought she was strange (which, to be fair, she was), and the ghosts, sensing their relatives' disapproval, gave Hildy the cold shoulder.

It was around this time that Hildy's parents died. *Perhaps* they *will be my ghost friends*, she thought, but no—they went off to find her dead sister and left Hildy all alone.

She hatched a new idea: she would sell her parents' house and buy a haunted one instead, which would have its own ghosts built in! So she went shopping for a new house. The real estate agent thought she was frustrating and strange (which, to be fair, she was) because every time she showed Hildy a perfectly nice house, Hildy's only question was whether anything terrible had ever happened there, like a murder or a suicide, or better yet a murder *and* a suicide, and she'd ignore the generous kitchen and light-filled drawing room to go look at the attic and basement.

Finally, she found a properly haunted house and bought it. It was only after she moved in, though, that she realized the ghost that came with it was only there part-time, stopping by every few nights to rattle chains and slam doors.

"Don't go," Hildy said, catching up to the ghost as he was leaving.

"Sorry, I have other houses to haunt," he replied, and hurried away.

Hildy felt cheated. She needed more than a part-time ghost. She'd gone to so much trouble to find a haunted house, but it seemed the one she bought wasn't haunted *enough*. She decided she needed the most haunted house in the world. She bought books about haunted houses and did research. She asked her part-time ghost what he knew, shouting questions after him as he raced from room to room, clanking here and slamming there. (He always seemed to be late for some more-important haunting, which Hildy tried not to take personally.) He said something about "Kwimbra," then left in a hurry. Hildy discovered that this was actually a town in Portugal—spelled *Coimbra*—and once she knew that, it was simple enough to track down which house in the town was most haunted. She exchanged letters with the man who lived there, in which he described being bothered day and night by disembodied screams and bottles that flew off tables, and she told him how pleasant that sounded. He thought this was strange, but also that she wrote very nicely, and when she offered to buy his house, his refusal was as gentle as could be. It had been in his family for generations, he explained, and so it had to remain. The house was his burden to bear.

Hildy was getting desperate. At a particularly low moment, she even entertained the thought of killing someone, because then their ghost would haunt her—but that didn't seem like a very good way to start a friendship, and she quickly abandoned the idea.

Finally, she decided that if she couldn't buy the most haunted house in the world, she would build it herself. First she chose the most haunted spot she could think of upon which to build it: the top of a hill that had been the site of a mass burial during the last outbreak of plague. Then she collected the most haunted building materials she could find: wood salvaged from a shipwreck with no survivors, bricks from a crematorium, stone columns from a poorhouse that had burned with hundreds of people inside, and windows from the palace of a mad prince who had poisoned his whole family. Hildy decorated the house with furniture, carpets, and objets d'art bought from other haunted houses, including that of the man in Portugal, who sent her a bureau from which emanated, at precisely three o'clock every morning, the sound of a crying baby. Just for good measure, she let bereaved families hold wakes in her parlor for an entire month, and then, just after the stroke of midnight in the middle of a howling rainstorm, she moved in.

Hildy was not disappointed—at least not right away. There were ghosts everywhere! In fact, there was hardly room in the house to hold them all. Ghosts crowded the basement and the attic, fought for space under the bed and in the closets, and there was always a line for the bathroom. (They didn't use the toilet, of course, but liked to check their hair in the mirror, to make sure it was disheveled and frightening.) They danced on the lawn at all hours—not because ghosts especially liked to dance, but because the people buried under the house had died of Dancing Plague.[2]

The ghosts clanked pipes and rattled windows and threw books down from shelves. Hildy walked from room to room introducing herself.

"You can see us?" asked the ghost of a young man. "And you aren't frightened?"

"Not at all," Hildy replied. "I like ghosts. Have you ever played stick-a-whack?"

"No, sorry," the ghost muttered, and turned away.

He seemed disappointed, as if all he'd wanted was to scare someone and she'd robbed him of the chance. So she pretended to be frightened by the next ghost she met, an old woman in the kitchen who was making knives float.

"Ahhhh!" Hildy cried. "What's happening to my knives! I must be losing my mind!"

---

2. Dancing Plague killed millions, but its victims invented the fox-trot, the Charleston, and the cha-cha slide. So, a mixed bag.

The old woman ghost seemed pleased, so she stepped back and raised her arms to make the knives float even higher—and then tripped over another ghost who was crawling on the floor behind her. The old lady ghost went sprawling and the knives clattered onto the counter.

"What do you think you're doing down there?" the old woman ghost shouted at the crawling ghost. "Can't you see I'm trying to work?"

"You should watch where you're going!" the crawling ghost shouted back.

"Watch where *I'm* going?"

Hildy started to laugh; she couldn't help it. The two ghosts stopped bickering and stared at her.

"I think she can see us," said the crawling ghost.

"Yes, obviously," said the old woman ghost. "And she isn't frightened in the least."

"No—I was!" Hildy said, stifling her laughter. "Honestly!"

The old woman ghost stood up and dusted herself off. "You're clearly humoring me," she said. "I've never been so humiliated in all my death."

Hildy didn't know what to do. She had tried being herself and that hadn't worked, and she'd tried acting like she thought the ghosts wanted her to, and that hadn't worked, either. Discouraged, she went to the hallway where the ghosts were lined up to use the bathroom and said, "Does anyone want to be my friend? I'm very nice, and I know lots of scary stories about living people that you might enjoy hearing." But the ghosts shuffled their feet and looked at the floor and said nothing. They could see her desperation, and it made them feel awkward.

After a long silence she slouched away, her face burning with embarrassment. She sat on the porch and watched the plague ghosts dance in the yard. It seemed she had failed. You can't force people to be friends with you—not even dead people.

Feeling ignored was even worse than feeling alone, so Hildy made plans to sell the house. The first five people who came to look at it were scared away before they even got through the front door. Hildy attempted to make the house somewhat less ghost-infested by selling some of the haunted furnishings back to their original owners. She wrote a letter to the man in Portugal asking if he'd be interested in taking back his wailing bureau. He replied straightaway. He didn't want the bureau, he said, but hoped she was doing well. And he signed the letter like this: *"Your friend, João."*

Hildy stared at the words for several minutes. Could she really call this man her friend? Or was he just being . . . friendly?

She wrote him back. She kept the tone of her letter light and breezy. She lied and told him she was doing fine, and asked how he was doing. She signed the letter like this: *"Your friend, Hildy."*

João and Hildy exchanged a few more letters. They were short and simple, just casual pleasantries and observations about the weather. Hildy still wasn't sure whether João actually considered her a friend or if he was just being polite. But then he closed a letter with this: "If you should ever find yourself in Coimbra, I would be honored if you paid me a visit."

She booked a rail ticket to Portugal that very day, packed a trunk full of clothes that night, and early the next morning a carriage arrived to whisk her off to the train station.

"Good-bye, ghosts!" she called out cheerfully from the front door. "I'll be back in a few weeks!"

The ghosts made no reply. She heard something shatter in the kitchen. Hildy shrugged and started toward the carriage.

It took a hot, dusty week of travel to reach João's house in Coimbra. During the long journey she tried to armor herself against inevitable disappointment. Hildy and João got along fine in letters, but she knew that in person he probably wouldn't like her, because no one did. She had to expect it or the pain of yet another rejection would surely crush her.

She arrived at his house, a spectral-looking mansion on a hill that seemed to watch her from cracked-window eyes. As Hildy walked toward its porch, a wave of black crows took off screaming from a dead oak in the front yard. She noticed a ghost swinging by a noose from the railing of the third-floor balcony, and waved to it. The ghost waved back, confused.

João answered the door and showed her inside. He was kind and gracious, and took Hildy's dusty traveling coat from her and laid out saucers of cinnamon-flavored milk tea and cakes. João made pleasant small talk, asking about her journey, about how the weather had been along the way, and about how they served tea where she came from. But Hildy kept tripping over her answers and felt absolutely sure she was making a fool of herself, and the more she thought about how foolish she sounded, the more difficult she found it to say anything at all. Finally, after an especially awkward silence, João asked, "Have I done something to offend you?" and Hildy knew she'd ruined the best chance she ever had to make a real friend. To hide the tears she felt coming, she got up from the table and ran into the next room.

João didn't come after her right away, but let Hildy have her privacy. She stood in the corner of his study and cried silently into her hands, furious at herself and so, so embarrassed. Then, after a few minutes, she heard a *thud* behind her and turned around. The ghost of a young girl was standing at a desk, knocking pens and paperweights onto the floor.

"Stop that," said Hildy, wiping away her tears. "You're making a mess of João's house."

"You can see me," the girl said.

"Yes, and I can see that you're far too old to be playing childish tricks on people."

"Yes, ma'am," the girl said, and disappeared through the wall.

"You spoke to it," said João, and Hildy was startled to see him watching from the doorway.

"Yes. I can see them, and talk to them. She won't bother you again— at least not today."

João was amazed. He sat and told Hildy about all the ways the ghosts had been making his life difficult—keeping him up at night, scaring away visitors, breaking his things. He'd tried to talk to them himself, but they never listened. Once he'd even called in a priest to get rid of them, but that had only made them angry, and they'd broken even more of his things the following night.

"You have to be firm with them, but understanding," Hildy explained. "It's not easy being a ghost, and like anyone, they want to feel respected."

"Do you think you could talk to them for me?" João asked meekly.

"I can certainly try," Hildy said. And then she realized that they'd been chatting for several minutes without a stumbled word or an awkward pause.

Hildy began that very day. The ghosts tried to hide from her, but she knew where they liked to go and coaxed each of them into the open to talk, one after another. Some of the talks went on for hours, with Hildy arguing and persisting while João looked on with quiet admiration. It took three days and nights, but in the end Hildy convinced most of the ghosts to leave the house, and asked the few who wouldn't to at least keep it down while João was sleeping and, if they must knock things off tables, to spare the family heirlooms.

João's house was transformed, and so was João. For three days and nights he had watched Hildy, and for three days and nights his feelings for her had deepened. Hildy had grown feelings for João, too. She found that she could talk to him easily about anything now, and was certain they were real friends. Even so, she was wary of seeming too eager and overstaying her welcome, and on the fourth day of her visit she packed her things and bid João good-bye. She had decided to go home, move to an unhaunted house, and try once more to make some living friends.

"I hope we'll see each other again," Hildy said. "I'll miss you, João. Perhaps you can come and visit *me* sometime."

"I'd like that," João said.

A carriage and driver were waiting to take Hildy to the train station. She waved good-bye and started toward the carriage.

"Wait!" João cried. "Don't go!"

Hildy stopped and turned to look at him. "Why?"

"Because I've fallen in love with you," João said.

The instant he said it, Hildy realized she loved him, too. And she ran back up the steps, and they threw their arms around each other.

At that, even the ghost that hung from the third-floor railing smiled.

Hildy and João got married, and Hildy moved into João's house. The few ghosts that remained were friendly to her, though she didn't need ghost friends anymore because now she had João. Before long they had a daughter and a son, too, and Hildy's life was fuller than she'd ever dreamed it could be. And as if that weren't enough, one fine midnight there was a knock on the front door, and who should Hildy find floating there on the porch but the ghosts of her sister and her parents.

"You came back!" Hildy cried, overjoyed.

"We came back a long time ago," her sister said, "but you'd moved away! It took forever to find you."

"No matter," Hildy's mother said. "We're together now!"

Then Hildy's two children came out onto the porch with João, wiping sleep from their eyes.

"Pai," said Hildy's little daughter to João, "why is Mamãe talking to the air?"

"She isn't," João said, and smiled at his wife. "Honey, is this who I think it is?"

Hildy hugged her husband with one arm and her sister with the other, and then, her heart so full she thought it might burst, she introduced her dead family to her living family.

And they lived happily ever after.

Cocobolo

—•—

s a boy, Zheng worshipped his father. This was during the reign of Kublai Khan in ancient China, long before Europe ruled the seas, and his father, Liu Zhi, was a famous ocean explorer. People said there was seawater in his blood. By the time he was forty, he'd achieved more than any mariner before him: he had mapped the whole eastern coast of Africa, made contact with unknown tribes in the heart of New Guinea and Borneo, and staked claim to extensive new territories for the empire. Along the way he had fought pirates and brigands, quelled a mutiny, and twice survived being shipwrecked. A great iron statue of him stood at Tianjin's harbor, gazing longingly at the sea. The statue was all Zheng had of his father, because the man himself disappeared when Zheng was just ten.

Liu Zhi's final expedition had been to discover the island of Cocobolo, long thought legendary, where it was said rubies grew on trees and liquid gold pooled in vast lakes. Before leaving, he told Zheng: "If I should never return, promise you'll come looking for me one day. Don't let grass grow under your feet!"

Zheng duly promised, thinking even the wild ocean could never best a man like his father—but Liu Zhi never came home. After a year with no word, the emperor held a lavish funeral in his honor. Zheng was inconsolable, and for days he wept at the feet of his father's statue. As he grew older, though, Zheng learned things about Liu Zhi that he had been too young to understand while the man was alive, and his opinion of his father slowly changed. Liu Zhi had been a strange man, and he'd grown even stranger near the end of his life. There were rumors he'd gone mad.

"He would go swimming in the sea for hours every day, even in winter," said Zheng's eldest brother. "He could hardly stand being on land."

"He thought he could talk to whales," said Zheng's uncle Ai, laughing. "Once I even heard him trying to speak their language!"

"He wanted us to go and live on an island in the middle of nowhere," said Zheng's mother. "I said to him, 'We banquet at the palace! We entertain dukes and viscounts! Why should we give up this life to live like savages in a sandpit?' He hardly spoke to me after that."

Liu Zhi had accomplished a great deal early in his life, people said, but then he'd begun chasing fantasies. He led a voyage to discover a land of talking dogs. He spoke of a place in the northernmost reaches of the Roman Empire where there lived shape-shifting women who could stop time.[1] He was shunned by polite society, and eventually the nobles stopped funding his expeditions—so he began funding them himself. When he'd exhausted his personal fortune, leaving his wife and children

---

1. It would seem that word of Britain's ymbrynes spread far and wide across the world, becoming the stuff of legend even among non-peculiars.

near bankruptcy, he dreamed up a mission to find Cocobolo in order to harvest its riches.

Zheng saw how his father's eccentricities had led to his downfall and, as he entered manhood, he was careful not to repeat Liu Zhi's mistakes. There was seawater in Zheng's blood, too, and like his father he became a mariner—but of a very different sort. He led no expeditions of discovery, no pioneering voyages to claim new lands for the empire. He was a thoroughly practical man, a merchant, and he oversaw a fleet of trading ships. He took no risks. He avoided routes favored by pirates and never strayed from familiar waters. And he was very successful.

His life on land was equally conventional. He banqueted at the palace and maintained friendships with all the right people. He never uttered a shocking word or held a controversial opinion. He was rewarded with social position and an advantageous marriage to the emperor's pampered grandniece, which put him within a hairbreadth of the nobility class.

To protect all he'd accumulated, he took pains to disassociate himself from his father. He never mentioned Liu Zhi. He changed his surname and pretended they weren't related. But the older Zheng got, the harder it became to push away his father's memory. Elderly relatives often made comments about how similar Zheng's mannerisms were to Liu Zhi's.

"The way you walk, the way you hold yourself," said his aunt Xi Pen. "Even the words you choose—it's as if he's standing before me!"

So Zheng attempted to change himself. He copied the loping gait of his older brother, Deng, whom no one ever compared to their father. Before he spoke, he paused to rearrange the words in his head and choose different ones that meant the same thing. He couldn't change his face, though, and every time he walked past the harbor, the giant statue of his father reminded Zheng just how much they resembled each other. So one night he snuck out to the harbor with a rope and a winch and, with a great deal of effort, he pulled the thing down.

On his thirtieth birthday, the dreams began. He was plagued by nighttime visions of the old man—starved and leathery, white beard to his knees, no longer resembling Zheng at all—waving desperately from the desert shore of some sunbaked island. Zheng would startle awake in the wee hours, sweat beading his brow, tormented by guilt. He'd made a promise to his father, one he'd never even attempted to fulfill.

Come and find me.

His herbalist prepared him a draught of strong medicine, which he took each night before bed, and it kept him sound asleep and dreamless until morning.

Shut out of his dreams, Zheng's father found other ways to haunt him.

Zheng found himself lingering by the docks one day, entertaining a mysterious impulse to jump into the ocean and go for a swim—in the middle of winter. He choked back the urge, and for weeks did not allow himself to even look at the sea.

A short time later he was captaining a voyage to Shanghai when, belowdecks, he heard the song of a whale. He put his ear to the hull and listened. For a moment he thought he could understand what the whale, in its long, unearthly vowels, was saying.

Co . . . co . . . bo . . . lo!

He plugged his ears with cotton, ran upstairs, and refused to go belowdecks again. He began to worry that he was losing his mind, just as his father had.

Back home on land, he had a new dream, one even his nightly draught of medicine could not suppress. In it, Zheng was bushwhacking through an island's tropical interior as rubies rained softly from the trees. The muggy air seemed to breathe his name—*Zheng, Zheng*—and though he could feel his father's presence all around him, he saw no one. Exhausted, he lay down in a patch of grass, and then suddenly it grew up around him, the sod peeling away from the earth to wrap him in a suffocating embrace.

He startled awake with his feet itching like mad. Throwing back the covers, he was alarmed to discover that they were covered in grass. He tried to brush it off, but every blade was connected to his feet. They were sprouting from his soles.

Terrified his wife would notice, Zheng leaped from the bed, ran to the bathroom, and shaved.

What on earth is happening to me? he thought to himself. The answer was clear enough: he was losing his mind, just as his father had.

The next morning, he awoke to find that not only had his feet sprouted grass again, but long ropes of seaweed had grown from his armpits. He raced into the bathroom, tore the seaweed out—it was very painful—and shaved his feet a second time.

The following day he awoke with the usual growths from his feet and armpits, as well as a new wrinkle: his bedsheets were full of sand. It had oozed from his pores in the night.

He went to the bathroom, ripped out the seaweed and shaved his feet, still convinced it was nothing but madness. But when he returned the sand was still in his bed, all over his wife, and in her hair. She was awake now, and very upset, trying in vain to shake it out.

If *she* could see it, Zheng realized, it had to be real. The sand, the

71

grass—all of it. Which meant he wasn't crazy after all. Something was *happening* to him.

Zheng went to see the herbalist, who gave him a foul-smelling poultice to rub all over his body. When that didn't help he went to a surgeon, who told him there was nothing to be done, aside from amputating his feet and plugging his pores with glue. That was obviously not acceptable, so he went to a monk and they prayed together, but Zheng fell asleep while praying and woke to find he'd leaked sand all over the monk's cell, and the angry monk kicked him out.

It seemed there was no cure for whatever was wrong with him, and the symptoms were only getting worse. The grass on his feet grew all the time now, not just at night, and the seaweed made him smell like a beach at low tide. His wife began sleeping in a separate bed in another room. He worried that his business associates would hear about his condition and shun him. That he would be ruined. In desperation, he began to entertain the idea of having his feet amputated and his pores plugged with glue—but then, in a sudden flash of memory, the last words his father had spoken to him came ringing in his ears.

Don't let grass grow under your feet.

Now that mysterious sentiment, which Zheng had wondered about for many years, made perfect sense. It had been a message—a coded message. His father had known this would happen to Zheng. He had known because it had also happened to him! They shared more than a face and a walk and a way of speaking—they shared this strange affliction, too.

Come and find me, he had said. *Don't let grass grow under your feet.*

Liu Zhi had not gone off to seek a mythical fortune. He had gone to find a *cure*. And if Zheng ever hoped to rid himself of this strangeness and live a normal life again, he would have to fulfill his promise to his father.

At dinner that evening, he announced his intentions to the family. "I'm mounting a voyage to find our father," he said.

They were incredulous. Others had tried and failed to find their father already, they reminded him. Searches had been financed by the emperor, but no trace of the man or his expedition had ever been found. Did he, a merchant who had never sailed anywhere but his safe trading routes, really expect to have better luck than they did?

"I can do it, you'll see," said Zheng. "I just have to find the island he went searching for."

"You would never find it even if you were the world's best navigator," said Aunt Xi. "How can you find a place that doesn't exist?"

Zheng left determined to prove his family wrong. The island *did* exist, and he knew just how to find it: he would stop taking his sleep medicine and let his dreams guide him. If that didn't work, he would listen to the whales!

His first mate tried to discourage him, too. Even if the island existed, he said, every mariner who had claimed to see it swore it couldn't be reached. They said it moved in the night. "How can you land on an island that runs away from you?" the first mate asked.

"By commissioning the fastest ship that's ever been built," Zheng replied.

Zheng spent the bulk of his fortune building that ship, which he named *Improbable*. It nearly bankrupted him, and he had to issue promissory notes to hire the crew.

His wife was livid. "You'll land us in the poorhouse!" she cried. "I'll have to take in laundry just to keep from starving!"

"I'll fill my pockets with rubies when I find Cocobolo," Zheng replied. "When I return I'll be richer than ever. You'll see!"

The *Improbable* set sail. It was rumored Cocobolo lay southwest of Ceylon in the Indian Ocean, but the island had never been spotted in the same place twice. Zheng stopped taking his sleep medicine and awaited prophetic dreams. In the meantime, the *Improbable* made for Ceylon.

Along the way they flagged down other vessels, seeking word of Cocobolo. "I saw it on the eastern horizon three weeks ago," said a fisherman, pointing into the blue. "Toward the Arabian Sea."

Zheng's sleep had been disappointingly dreamless, so they sailed east. In the Arabian Sea they met a ship captain who told them he'd spotted it two weeks prior. "In the west, near Sumatra," he said.

By then Zheng had begun dreaming, but the dreams had been meaningless—so they sailed west. At Sumatra, a man shouted down from a sea cliff that Cocobolo had been seen in the southeast, near Thinadhoo. "You just missed it," he said.

And so the voyage went for several months. The crew became restless, and there were whispers of mutiny. The first mate urged Zheng to give up.

"If the island was real, we would have found it by now," he said.

Zheng pleaded for more time. He spent that night praying for prophetic dreams, and the next day belowdecks with his ear pressed to the hull wall, straining to hear whale song. Neither songs nor dreams came to him, and Zheng began to despair. If he returned home empty-handed, he'd be flat broke and still without a cure. His wife would surely leave him. His family would shun him. His investors would refuse to back him, and his business would fail.

He stood at the bow of the ship, discouraged, and gazed down into the churning green water. He felt a sudden, strong urge to go for a swim. This time, he did not suppress it.

He hit the water with incredible force. The current was strong and shockingly cold, and it pulled him down.

He did not fight it. He felt himself drowning.

From out of the darkness emerged a giant eye suspended in a wall of gray flesh. It was a whale, and it was moving toward him rapidly. Before it could collide with him, the whale dove and disappeared from view. Then, just as suddenly, Zheng's feet connected with something solid. The whale was pushing from below, propelling him upward.

They broke the surface together. Zheng coughed up a lungful of water. Someone from the ship threw him a rope. He tied it around his waist, and as he was being pulled back on board, he heard the whale singing below him.

Its song said: *follow me.*

As he was pulled onto the deck, Zheng saw the whale swim away. Though he was trembling from cold and struggling for breath, he found the strength to shout, "Follow that whale!"

The *Improbable* trimmed its sails and gave chase. They followed the whale all that day and through the night, marking its position by the mist from its blowhole. When the sun rose, there was an island on the horizon—one that did not appear on the map.

It could only be Cocobolo.

They sailed toward it as fast as the wind would take them, and throughout the day what had been a mere speck on the horizon grew larger and larger. But night fell before they could reach it, and when the sun rose again the island was but a speck in the distance.

"It's just as they said," Zheng marveled. "It *moves.*"

They chased the island for three days. Each day they drew tantalizingly close to it, only for it to slip away each night. Then a strong wind pushed them toward the island faster than ever, and finally the *Improbable* was able to reach it, anchoring in a sandy cove just as the sun was dipping toward the horizon.

Zheng had been dreaming of Cocobolo for months, and he'd let his dreams run a bit wild. Reality was nothing like what he'd envisioned: there were no waterfalls of gold pouring into the sea, no mountain slopes glimmering with ruby-laden trees. It was a lumpy collection of unremarkable hills covered with dense greenery, exactly like a thousand islands he'd passed in his travels. Most disappointingly, there was no sign of his father's expedition. He'd imagined finding his ship half sunk in a cove, and the old man himself, twenty years a castaway, waiting for him on a beach, cure in hand. But there was only a crescent of white sand and a wall of waving palm trees.

The ship dropped anchor, and Zheng splashed ashore with his first mate and a detachment of armed crewmen. He told himself it was too soon to be disappointed, but after several hours of searching they had found neither Liu Zhi nor any sign of human settlement, and Zheng was more disappointed than ever.

The light had begun to fade. They were about to make camp when they heard a rustle in the trees. A pair of jaguars burst through the undergrowth and let out a terrifying roar.

The men scattered. They shot arrows at the jaguars, which only seemed to enrage the cats further. One leaped at Zheng and he ran for his life. He barreled through the jungle until his lungs were burning and his clothes had been shredded by the undergrowth, and then he stopped. Once his breathing had quieted he listened for his men, but heard nothing. He was alone and lost and it was nearly dark.

He looked for shelter. After a while he came upon a cluster of caves. A hot, humid wind was passing in and out of them at regular intervals. He thought it was as good a place as any to wait out the night, and ducked inside.

He dug a small pit and made a fire. No sooner had the flames started to rise than the ground convulsed beneath him and a deafening cry echoed up from the depths of the cave.

"Put it out! Put the fire out!" the voice boomed.

Terrified, Zheng kicked dirt onto the flames. As the fire died, the ground beneath him stopped shaking.

"Why do you hurt me?" said the powerful voice. "What did I ever do to you?"

Zheng didn't know to whom he was speaking, only that he'd better reply. "I didn't mean to hurt anyone!" he said. "I only wanted to cook some food."

"Well, how would you like it if I dug a hole in *your* skin and lit a fire?"

Zheng's gaze fell upon the extinguished fire pit, which he saw was quickly filling with liquid gold.

"Who are you?" the voice demanded.

"My name is Zheng. I hail from the port city of Tianjin."

There was a long silence, and then a gale of hearty laughter rolled up from the cave. "You've come at last!" the voice said. "I can't tell you how happy I am to see you, dear boy!"

"I don't understand," said Zheng. "Who are you?"

"Why, don't you recognize your father's voice?"

"My father!" Zheng cried, turning to look behind him. "Where?"

There was another peal of laughter from the cave. "All around you!" said the voice, and then a lump of earth rose up beside him and wrapped him in a sandy embrace. "How terribly I've missed you, Zheng!"

With a shock, Zheng realized that he was not talking to some giant hiding inside the cave, but to the cave itself. "You're not my father!" he cried, squirming out of its grasp. "My father is a man—a human!"

"I *was* a human," said the voice. "I've changed quite a bit, as you can see. But I'll always be your father."

"You're trying to trick me. Your name is Cocobolo—you move in the night and liquid gold puddles in your holes. That's what the legends say."

"The same things are true of any man who becomes an island."

"There are others like you?"

"Here and there.[2] Cocobolo isn't just one island, you see. We are all Cocobolo. But I am your father."

"I'll believe you if you can prove it," said Zheng. "What were the last words you said to me?"

"Come and find me," said the voice. "And don't let grass grow under your feet."

Zheng fell to his knees and wept. It was true: his father was the island, and the island was his father. The caves were his nose and mouth, the earth his skin, the grass his hair. The gold filling the pit Zheng had dug was his blood. If his father had come here seeking a cure, he'd failed

---

2. Living islands are virtually unknown in peculiardom today. If any still exist, they stay very well hidden. No one can blame them for being shy—historically, such islands have been mined for their blood, a process every bit as grotesque and painful as it sounds.

to find one—and so had Zheng. He felt desperate and hopeless. Is *this* what he was doomed to become?

"Oh, Father, it's awful, it's awful!"

"It isn't awful," his father replied, sounding a bit injured. "I *like* being an island."

"You do?"

"It took a bit of getting used to, of course, but it's infinitely better than the alternative."

"And what's so bad about being human?" It was Zheng's turn to feel insulted.

"Nothing at all," his father said, "if human is what you're meant to be. I myself was not meant to be human forever, though for many years I couldn't accept it. I fought hard against the changes that were overtaking me—and which are also overtaking you. I solicited the help of doctors, and when they proved useless I sought out distant cultures and consulted their sorcerers and witch doctors, but no one could make it stop. I was unutterably miserable. Finally, I couldn't take it anymore and I left home, found a distant patch of ocean in which to live, and allowed my sand to spread and my grass to grow—and heavens, it was such a relief."

"And you're really happy like this?" said Zheng. "A smudge of jaguar-infested jungle in the middle of the sea?"

"I am," his father replied. "Though I admit being an island is lonely sometimes. The only other Cocobolo in this part of the world is a tiresome old crank, and the only humans who visit me want to drain my blood. But if my son were here alongside me—ah, I'd want for nothing!"

"I'm sorry," said Zheng, "but that isn't why I've come. I don't want to be an island, I want to be normal!"

"But you and I *aren't* normal," said his father.

"You gave up too soon, that's all. There must be a cure!"

"No, son," said the island, letting out a sigh of such force that it blew Zheng's hair back. "There is no cure. This is our natural form."

To Zheng this news was worse than a death sentence. Overwhelmed by hopelessness and anger, he raged and wept. His father tried to console him. He raised a bed of soft grass for Zheng to lie on. When it began to rain, he bent the palms so that they sheltered him. After Zheng exhausted himself and fell asleep, his father kept the jungle cats at bay with frightening rumbles.

When Zheng woke in the morning, he had moved past hopelessness. There was an iron will inside him, and it refused to accept the loss of his humanity. He would fight for it, cure or no cure, and if need be he would fight to the death. As for his father, just thinking about him made Zheng unbearably sad—so he resolved never to think of him again.

He gathered himself up and started to walk away.

"Wait!" his father said. "Please stay and join me. We'll be islands together, you and me—a little archipelago!—and we'll always have each other's company. It's fate, son!"

"It's not fate," Zheng said bitterly. "You made a choice." And he marched off into the jungle.

His father didn't try and stop him, though he easily could have. A sorrowful moan rose up from his cave mouth, along with waves of hot breath that swept across the island. As he wept, the boughs of trees shivered and shook, releasing a soft rain of rubies from their branches. Zheng, pausing here and there to scoop them up, filled his pockets, and by the time he'd reached the cove and rejoined his ship, he'd collected enough of his father's tears to pay all his men's salaries and fill his empty coffers back home.

His men cheered when they saw him, having thought him killed by jaguars, and on his order they reeled up their anchor and set sail for Tianjin.

"What about your father?" his first mate asked, taking Zheng aside to speak privately.

"I'm satisfied that he's dead," Zheng replied tersely, and the mate nodded and asked no more about it.

Even as Cocobolo receded into the distance behind them, Zheng could still hear his father weeping. Fighting a powerful swell of regret, he stood at the bow and refused to look back.

For a day and a night, a pod of minke whales rode the *Improbable*'s wake, singing to him.

> *Don't go.*
>
> *Don't go.*
>
> *You are Cocobolo's son.*

He plugged his ears and did his best to ignore them.

During the long voyage home, Zheng became obsessed with suppressing the transformation that was happening to him. He shaved his feet and trimmed the seaweed growing from his armpits. His skin was nearly always dusted with the fine, powdery sand that his pores exuded, so he took to wearing high collars and long sleeves, and bathed every morning in seawater.

The day he arrived home, even before going to see his wife, Zheng went to his surgeon. He instructed the man to do anything necessary to halt his transformation. The surgeon gave Zheng a powerful sleeping draught, and when Zheng awoke he found that his armpits had been filled with sticky tar, his skin covered in glue to stop up his pores, and his feet amputated and replaced with wooden ones. Zheng regarded himself in a mirror and was filled with revulsion. He looked bizarre. Still, he was grimly optimistic that the sacrifice he'd made had saved his humanity, and he paid the doctor and hobbled home on his new wooden feet.

When his wife saw him, she nearly fainted. "What have you done to yourself?" she cried.

He invented a lie about being injured while saving a man's life at sea, and to explain the gluey skin, something about a bad reaction to the tropical sun. He repeated the same lies to his family and his business associates, along with another about finding his father's body on Cocobolo.[3] Liu Zhi, he told them, was dead. They were more interested in the rubies he'd brought back.

For a time, life was good. His bizarre growths had stopped. Hobbling about on wooden feet, he had traded a freakish affliction for a relatively mundane one, and he could live with that. The rubies had brought him fame not only as a rich man but also as an explorer: he had discovered Cocobolo and returned to tell the story. There were banquets and parties in his honor.

Zheng tried to convince himself he was happy. In the hopes it might strangle the small voice of regret that mewled inside him now and then, he tried to convince himself that his father really was dead. *It was all in your mind,* he told himself. *That island could not really have been your father.*

But sometimes, when his business took him down by the harbor, he thought he could still hear the song of the whales, calling him back to Cocobolo. Sometimes, while looking at the ocean through a spyglass, he

---

3. Technically it wasn't a lie, since his father's body *was* Cocobolo.

swore he could see a familiar smudge on the horizon that was not a ship, and where no island was mapped. Gradually, over the course of weeks, he felt a strange pressure building inside him. He felt it most severely when he was near water: it seemed to remind his body of what it wanted to become. If he stood at the end of a dock and filled his gaze with the ocean, he could feel the grass and sand and seaweed he'd locked inside himself straining to get out.

He stopped going near the water. He vowed never to set foot on board a ship again. He bought a house far inland, where he would never have to glimpse the ocean. But even that was not enough: he felt the pressure every time he bathed or washed his face or got caught in the rain. So he stopped bathing and washing his face, and he never went outside if there was even a single dark cloud in the sky. He would not even drink a cup of water, for fear it might ignite in him desires he couldn't control. When he absolutely needed to, he sucked on a wet cloth.

"Not a drop," he told his wife. "I won't allow a single drop in this house."

And so it went. Many years passed without Zheng touching water. Old and dry as dust, Zheng came to resemble a very large raisin, but neither his growths nor his desires returned. He and his wife never had children, in part because Zheng was glued shut from top to bottom, but also because he feared passing his affliction on to another generation.

One day, in order to make out a will, Zheng was sorting through his personal effects. In the bottom of a drawer he came upon a small silk bag, and when he upended it, a ruby fell into his palm. He'd sold the rest long ago and had thought this one lost, and yet here it was, cool and heavy in his hand. Before that moment, he had not thought of his father in half a lifetime.

His hands began to tremble. He hid the ruby out of sight and turned to other business, but he could not seem to stop what was welling up inside him.

Where the moisture was coming from he could not imagine. He had not even sucked on a rag in three days, but his vision began to blur and his eyes to well, as if some secret reserve inside him were being tapped.

"No!" he shouted, slamming his fists down on the table. "No, no, no!"

He looked desperately around the room for something to distract his mind. He counted backward from twenty. He sang a nonsensical song. But nothing would stop it.

When it finally happened, the event was so anticlimactic he wondered if he hadn't made too much of it. A tear tracked down his cheek, rolled off his chin, and fell to the floor. He stood frozen, staring at the dark splotch it made on the wood.

For a long moment, all was still and quiet. Then, the thing Zheng feared most happened. It began with that old, terrible pressure within him, which in a matter of moments became unbearable. It felt as if his body were having an earthquake.

The glue that covered him cracked and fell away. Sand began to pour from his skin. The tar that had stopped up his armpits disintegrated, and ropes of seaweed shot out of him at an incredible rate. In less than a minute, it had nearly filled the room he was in, and he knew he had to get out of his house or it would be destroyed. He ran outside— and into a driving rainstorm.

He fell down in the middle of the street, sand and seaweed gushing out of him. People who saw him ran away screaming. His wooden feet blew off, and from their stumps rushed endless lengths of grass. His body began to grow, the rain and the grass mixing with the sand to form earth, layers and layers of which wrapped around him like skin upon skin. Soon he was as wide as the street and as tall as his house.

A mob formed and attacked him. Zheng struggled to stand on his grassy stumps and then to run. He fell, crushing a house under his weight. He stood again and lumbered on, laboring up a hill with thundering steps that punched holes in the street.

The mob chased him, joined by soldiers who fired arrows at his back. From his wounds gushed liquid gold, which only encouraged more people to join the attack. All the while, Zheng was steadily growing, and soon he was twice the width of his street and three times the height of his house. His form was fast becoming inhuman, his arms and legs disappearing within the giant, earthen ball that was his midsection.

He made it to the top of the street on tiny, waddling stumps. A moment later they were swallowed up, and with nothing left to steady him, his round form began to roll down the other side—slowly at first, then faster and faster. He became unstoppable, flattening houses and wagons and people as he went, growing larger all the while.

He careened into the harbor, hurtled down a splintering dock, and then splashed into the sea, making a wave so big that all the boats around him swamped. Submerged and drifting, he began to grow faster than ever, his grass and earth and sand and seaweed spreading over the water to form a small island. The transformation was so all-consuming that he did not notice the approach of several of the emperor's warships. He felt it, though, when they began to fire their cannons into him.

The pain was incredible. His blood made the sea shine golden in the sun. He thought his life was about to end—until he heard a familiar voice.

It was his father, calling his name.

Cocobolo plowed into their midst with a great rumble. The wake he made knocked over the emperor's warships like they were toys. Zheng felt something link with him beneath the surface of the water, and then his father was pulling him out to sea. Once they were away from danger and all was quiet, his father used bent coconut palms to catapult earth into the holes that had been shot through Zheng.

"Thank you," Zheng said, his voice a loud rumble that came from he knew not where. "I don't deserve your kindness."

"Of course you do," replied his father.

"You were keeping watch," said Zheng.

"Yes," said his father.

"For all these years?"

"Yes," he said again. "I had a feeling you'd need my help one day."

"But I was so cruel to you."

His father was quiet for a moment. Then he said: "You're my son."

Zheng's bleeding had stopped, but now he felt a worse pain: incredible shame. Zheng was well acquainted with shame, but this type was new. He was ashamed by the kindness he'd been shown. He was ashamed at how he'd treated his poor father. But he was ashamed, most of all, of how ashamed he'd been of himself, and of what he'd let that turn him into.

"I'm sorry, Father." Zheng wept. "I'm so very sorry."

Even as he cried, Zheng could feel himself growing, his sand and grass and earth creeping outward, his seaweed thickening into a forest of submarine kelp. The coral reef that encircled his father linked itself to the one beginning to form around Zheng, and with a gentle tug, the elder Cocobolo led the younger still farther out to sea.

"There's a wonderful spot near Madagascar where we can relax in safety," said the elder. "I believe you need a nice, long nap."

Zheng let himself be pulled along and, as the days passed, he began to feel something wonderful and entirely new.

He felt like himself.

The Pigeons of Saint Paul's

Editor's note:

The story of the pigeons and their cathedral is one of the oldest in peculiar folklore, and it has taken drastically different forms over the centuries. While the most common versions cast the pigeons as builders, I find their role as destroyers in this iteration much more interesting.

—MN

nce upon a peculiar time, long before there were towers or steeples or tall buildings of any sort in the city of London, all the pigeons lived high up in the trees where they could keep away from the bustle and fracas of human society. They didn't care for the way humans smelled or the strange noises they made with their mouths or the mess they made of things generally, but they did appreciate the perfectly edible things they dropped on the street and threw into garbage heaps. Thus, the pigeons liked to stay near humans, but not *too* near. Twenty to forty feet above their heads was just about perfect.

But then London started to grow—not just outward, but upward—and the humans began building lookout towers and churches with steeples and other things that intruded upon what the pigeons considered their private domain. So the pigeons called a meeting, and several thousand of them gathered on an empty island in the middle of the river Thames[1] to decide what to do about the humans and their increasingly tall buildings. Pigeons being democratic, speeches were made and the question was put to a vote. A small contingent voted to put up with the humans and share the air. A smaller faction advocated leaving London altogether and finding somewhere less crowded to live. But the vast majority voted to declare war.

Of course, the pigeons knew they couldn't win a war against humans—nor did they want to. (Who would drop scraps for them to eat if the humans were dead?) But pigeons are experts in the art of sabotage, and with a clever combination of disruption and vandalism, they began a centuries-long fight to keep the humans at ground level, where they belonged. In the beginning it was easy because the humans built everything from wood and straw. Just a few burning embers deposited in a thatch roof could reduce an annoyingly tall building to ashes. But the humans kept rebuilding—they were bafflingly un-discourageable—and the pigeons continued to torch any structure taller than two stories just as fast as the humans could erect them.

Eventually the humans grew wiser and began building their towers and steeples from stone, which made them much harder to burn down—so the pigeons tried to disrupt their construction instead. They pecked

---

1. Known today as Eel Pie Island, it has long been a meeting place for the peculiar. It was a favorite haunt of King Henry VIII, and in the twentieth century, hippies, anarchists, and rock musicians flocked there.

at workers' heads, knocked down scaffolding, and pooped on architectural plans. This slowed the humans' progress a bit, but didn't stop it, and after some years a great stone cathedral rose higher than any of the trees in London. The pigeons considered it an eyesore and an affront to their dominance of the sky. It made them terribly grumpy.

Happily, Vikings soon raided the city and tore it down—along with most of London. The pigeons loved the Vikings, who didn't care for tall buildings and left tasty garbage all over the place. But after some years the Vikings went away and the steeple-builders got to work again. They chose a high hill overlooking the river and constructed a massive cathedral there, one that dwarfed everything that had come before it. They named it Saint Paul's. Time and time again the pigeons tried to burn it down, but the humans had dedicated a small army of firefighters to the protection of the cathedral, and the pigeons' every effort was thwarted.

Frustrated and angry, the pigeons began setting fires in adjacent neighborhoods, at places upwind from the cathedral on gusty nights, in hopes the flames would spread. Early on the morning of September 2, 1666, their efforts were disastrously successful. A pigeon named Nesmith set fire to a bakery a half mile from Saint Paul's. As the bakery was consumed, a ferocious wind pushed the flames straight uphill toward the cathedral. It burned completely—naves, belfries, and all—and after four days of destruction, so had eighty-seven other churches and more than ten thousand homes. The city was a smoking ruin.[2]

The pigeons hadn't envisioned such devastation, and they felt

---

2. Some accounts of the fire even have the pigeons fanning the flames with their wings. Truly a shameful moment in peculiar history.

genuinely bad about it. Emotionally, it was a different thing altogether from the Viking raids. Though the damage was comparable, this was their fault entirely. They called a meeting and debated whether to leave London altogether. Perhaps, some argued, they did not deserve to live there anymore. The vote was split, and they decided to return the following day and debate the matter again. That night the revenge attacks began. There was a contingent of humans who seemed to understand that pigeons were to blame for the fire, and had decided to drive them out. They soaked bread crumbs in arsenic and tried to poison the pigeons. They cut down the pigeons' favorite roosting trees and destroyed their nests. They chased pigeons with brooms and bats and shot at them with muskets. After that, not a single pigeon was willing to leave the city; they were too proud. Instead they voted to fight back again.

The pigeons pecked and pooped and spread disease and did everything they could to make the humans miserable. In turn, the humans ratcheted up their violence against the birds. Truthfully, the pigeons couldn't do much more than annoy the humans, but when the humans started to rebuild the cathedral—the very symbol of their arrogance—the pigeons waged all-out war. Thousands of them descended on the construction site, risking life and wing to chase away the workers. Day after day, pitched battles were waged between the humans and the birds, and no matter how many pigeons the humans killed, more always seemed to come. They reached a stalemate. Construction ground to a halt; it seemed there would never be another cathedral on the site of Saint Paul's, and that the pigeons of London would be harassed and killed forever.

A year passed. The pigeons continued to fight, and their numbers to dwindle, and though the humans were steadily rebuilding the rest of London, they seemed to have abandoned their plans for the cathedral. Yet the violence continued, because hatred between humans and pigeons had become ingrained.

One day, the pigeons were meeting on their island when a rowboat arrived carrying a single human. The pigeons became alarmed and were about to swarm him when he raised his arms and shouted, "I come in peace!" They soon learned that he wasn't like most other humans—haltingly, brokenly, he could speak the pigeons' native language of chirps and coos. He knew a great deal about birds, he told them, and peculiar birds at that, because his mother had been one. Moreover, he sympathized with their cause and wanted to broker a peace.

The pigeons were astounded. They took a vote and decided not to peck the man's eyes out—at least not right away. They questioned him. The man's name was Wren, and he was an architect. His fellow humans had tasked him with attempting to rebuild the cathedral on the hill yet again.

"You're wasting your time," said Nesmith, the fire starter and the pigeons' leader. "Too many of us have died to prevent it."

"Of course, nothing can be built without peace," replied Wren, "and no peace can be achieved without understanding. I come seeking a new understanding between my kind and yours. First: we recognize that the air is your domain, and we will build nothing in it without your permission."

"And why would we give our permission?"

"Because this new building would be different from all the ones that came before. It would not be meant solely for the use of humans. It would be yours, too."

Nesmith laughed. "And what would we want with a building?"

"Why, Nesmith," said another pigeon, "if we had a building we could escape from the cold and the rain when the weather was bad. We could roost and lay eggs and stay warm."

"Not with humans around to bother us!" replied Nesmith. "We need a space all our own."

"What if I could promise you that?" said Wren. "I'll make the cathedral so tall that humans won't have any interest in using the top half at all."

Wren did more than make promises. He returned day after day to discuss his plans, and even altered them to satisfy the pigeons' whims. They demanded all sorts of nooks and crannies and belfries and arches that were all but useless to humans, but were cozier than a living room to pigeons, and Wren agreed. He even promised the pigeons their own entrance, high above the ground and inaccessible to the non-winged. In exchange, the pigeons promised not to stand in the way of construction, and once it was built, not to make too much noise during services or poop on the worshippers.

And so an historic accord was forged. The pigeons and humans called off their war and returned to merely annoying one another. Wren built his cathedral—*their* cathedral—a proud and towering place, and the pigeons never again tried to destroy it. In fact, they felt such pride in Saint Paul's that they swore to protect it—and to this day they still do. When fires break out they swarm and beat the flames with their wings. They chase away vandals and thieves. During the great war, squadrons of pigeons redirected bombs in midair so that they fell clear of the building. It's safe to say that Saint Paul's would not be standing today without its winged caretakers.

Wren and the pigeons became lifelong friends. For the rest of his life, England's most esteemed architect never went anywhere without a pigeon close at hand to advise him. Even after he died, the birds went to visit him, now and again, in the land below. To this day, you'll find the cathedral they built still towering over London, peculiar pigeons keeping watch.

95

The Girl Who Could Tame Nightmares

nce there was a girl named Lavinia who wanted nothing more than to become a doctor like her father. She had a kind heart and a sharp mind and she loved helping people. She would have made an excellent doctor— but her father insisted it wasn't possible. He had a kind heart, too, and merely wanted to save his daughter from disappointment; at that time there were no female doctors in America at all. It seemed inconceivable that she would be accepted to a medical school, so he urged her toward more practical ambitions. "There are other ways to help people," he told her. "You could be a teacher."

But Lavinia hated her teachers. At school, while the boys were learning science, Lavinia and the other girls were taught how to knit and cook. But Lavinia would not be discouraged. She stole the boys' science books and memorized them. She spied through the keyhole as her father examined patients in his office, and she pestered him with endless questions about his work. She sliced open frogs she'd caught in the yard to examine their insides. One day, she vowed, she would discover a cure for something. One day she would be famous.

She could never have guessed how soon that day would arrive, or in what form. Her younger brother, Douglas, had always suffered from bad dreams, and lately they'd been getting worse. He often woke up screaming, convinced that monsters were coming to eat him.

"There are no monsters," Lavinia said, comforting him one night. "Try thinking about some baby animals as you fall asleep, or Cheeky romping in a field." She patted their old bloodhound, who lay curled at the foot of the bed. So Douglas tried thinking of Cheeky and baby chickens as he fell asleep the following night, but in his dreams the dog turned into a monster that bit the chicks' heads off, and he woke up screaming once again.

Concerned that Douglas might be ill, their father looked in Douglas's eyes and ears and throat and checked him all over for rashes, but he could find nothing physically wrong with the boy. The night terrors got so bad that Lavinia decided to examine Douglas herself, just in case their father had missed something.

"But you're not a doctor," Douglas protested. "You're just my sister."

"Hush up and hold still," she said. "Now go *ahhh*."

She peered into his throat, his nose, and his ears—and deep inside the latter, with the aid of a light, she spied a mass of strange black stuff. She poked her finger in and wiggled it about, and when she removed it, a string of sooty, threadlike stuff was wrapped around the tip. As she pulled her hand away, three long feet of it unraveled from Douglas's ear.

"Hey, that tickles!" he said, laughing.

She balled the thread in her hand. It squirmed, ever so slightly, as if alive.

Lavinia showed it to her father. "How strange," he remarked, holding it up to a light.

"What is it?" she asked.

"I'm not sure," he said, frowning. The thread was wriggling slowly out of his hand toward Lavinia. "I think it likes you, though."

"Perhaps it's a new discovery!" she said excitedly.

"I doubt it," her father said. "In any case, it's nothing for you to worry about." He patted her on the head, put the thread into a drawer, and locked it.

"I'd like to examine it, too," she said.

"It's time for lunch," he replied, shooing her out.

She stomped away to her room, annoyed. That might have been the end of it, if not for this: Douglas had no nightmares that night or any night after, and he credited his recovery entirely to Lavinia.

Their father wasn't so sure. A short time later, though, a patient of his complained of insomnia due to bad dreams, and when nothing the doctor prescribed seemed to help, he reluctantly asked Lavinia to take a look in the patient's ear. Just eleven and small for her age, she had to stand on a chair to see in. Sure enough, it was clogged with a mass of thready black stuff, which her father had not been able to see. She stuck her pinkie inside, wiggled it around, then wound out a thread from the patient's ear. It was so long and so thoroughly attached to the inside of his head that, to pull it loose, she had to climb down from her stool, dig her heels into the floor, and yank with both hands. When it finally snapped free of his head, she fell backward onto the floor and the patient tumbled off the examination table.

Her father snatched up the black thread and stuffed it into his drawer with the other batch.

"But it's *mine*," Lavinia protested.

"It's his, actually," said her father, helping the man up from the floor. "Now go and play with your brother."

The man returned three days later. He hadn't had a single nightmare since Lavinia had removed the thread from his ear.

"Your daughter is a miracle worker!" he declared, speaking to Lavinia's father but beaming straight at her.

As word of Lavinia's mysterious talent spread, their house began to receive a steady stream of visitors, all of whom wanted Lavinia to take away their nightmares. Lavinia was thrilled; perhaps this was how she was meant to help people. [1]

But her father turned them all away, and when she demanded to know why, all he would say was, "It's unbecoming for a lady to stick her fingers into strangers' ears."

Lavinia suspected another reason for his disapproval, however: more people were coming to see Lavinia than her father. He was *jealous*.

Bitter and frustrated, Lavinia bided her time. As luck would have it, a few weeks later her father was called away on urgent business. It was an unexpected trip and he hadn't had time to arrange for someone to watch the children.

"Promise me you won't . . ." her father said, and pointed at his ear. (He didn't know what to call the thing she did, and didn't like talking about it in any case.)

---

1. There are many dream-manipulators in peculiar history, but only one who shared Lavinia's talent for making real the immaterial stuff of dreams. His name was Cyrus and he was a thief of pleasant dreams: he needed them to survive, and became infamous for stealing the happiness of entire towns, one night and one house at a time.

"I promise," Lavinia said, fingers crossed behind her back.

The doctor kissed his children, hefted his bags, and went. He'd only been gone a few hours when there was a knock at the door. Lavinia opened it to find a miserable young woman standing on the porch, pale as death, her haunted-looking eyes ringed by dark circles. "Are you the one who can take away nightmares?" she asked meekly.

Lavinia showed her in. Her father's office was locked, so Lavinia brought the young woman into the sitting room, laid her down on the couch, and proceeded to pull a huge quantity of black thread from her ear. When she was finished the young woman wept with gratitude. Lavinia gave her a handkerchief, refused any payment, and showed her to the door.

After she'd gone, Lavinia turned to see Douglas watching from the hall. "Papa told you not to," he said sternly.

"That's my business, not yours," Lavinia answered. "You're not going to tell him, are you?"

"I might," he said nastily. "I haven't decided."

"If you do, I'll put these right back where I found them!" She held up the wad of nightmare thread and made as if to stick it in Douglas's ear, and he fled from the room.

As she stood there, feeling slightly bad for having scared him, the thread in her hand rose up like a charmed snake and pointed down the hall.

"What is it?" she said. "Are we going somewhere?"

She followed its lead. When she came to the end of the hall, it turned and nodded left—toward her father's office. Arriving at the locked door, the little thread strained toward the lock. Lavinia lifted it up and let it worm inside the keyhole, and a few moments later the door came open with a click.

"My goodness," she said. "You're a clever little nightmare, aren't you?"

She slipped inside and closed the door. The thread slid out of the lock, dropped into her hand, then pointed across the room toward the drawer where her father had stashed the other threads. It wanted to be with its friends!

She felt briefly guilty, then chased the feeling away—they were only reclaiming her rightful property, after all. Crossing to the drawer, her thread repeated its trick on the padlock that secured it, and the drawer slid open. Upon seeing each other, the new thread and the old tensed and reared back. They circled each other on the desk, tentative, sniffing each other like dogs. Then each seemed to decide the other was friendly, and in a blur they meshed together to form a fist-sized ball.

Lavinia laughed and clapped her hands. How fascinating! How delightful!

All day long people came to the door seeking Lavinia's help: a mother tormented by dreams of a lost child; small kids brought by anxious parents; an old man who each night relived scenes from a bloody war he'd fought half a century ago. She drew out dozens of nightmares and added them to the ball. After three days the ball was as large as a watermelon. After six it was nearly the size of their dog, Cheeky, who bared his teeth and growled whenever he saw it. (When the ball growled back, Cheeky dove out an open window and didn't come back.)

At night she stayed up late studying the ball. She prodded and poked it and studied bits of it under a microscope. She pored over her father's medical textbooks looking for any mention of thread that lived inside the ear canal, but found nothing. It meant she had made a scientific breakthrough—that, perhaps, Lavinia *herself* was a breakthrough!

Beside herself with excitement, she dreamed of opening a clinic where she would use her talent to help people. Everyone from paupers to presidents would come to see her, and one day, perhaps, nightmares would be a thing of the past! The thought made her so happy that for days she was practically walking on air.

Her brother, meanwhile, spent most of his time avoiding her. The ball made him deeply uncomfortable—the way it stayed in constant, wriggling motion even while sitting still; the subtle but pervasive smell it gave off of rotten eggs; the low, steady hum it made, impossible to ignore at night when there was no other noise in the house. The way it followed his sister everywhere, nipping at her heels like a devoted pet: up and down the stairs, to bed, to the dinner table, where it waited patiently for scraps—even to the bathroom, bumping against the door until she came out.[2]

"You should get rid of that thing," Douglas told her. "It's just trash from people's heads."

"I like having Baxter around," Lavinia said.

"You *named* it?"

Lavinia shrugged. "I think he's cute."

But the truth was Lavinia didn't know how to get rid of him. Lavinia had tried locking Baxter in a trunk so she could walk into town without him rolling after her, but he had broken open the lid. She had shouted and raged at him, but Baxter had simply bounced in place, excited for the attention he was being paid. She had even tried tying him in a sack,

103

---

2. Much has been made of this passage, which some read as evidence that Lavinia's nightmare ball is demonic in origin, and that Lavinia herself is a sort of dream exorcist. Personally, I think that's silly, and that some so-called academics watch too many horror movies in their spare time. The ball merely has a few unpleasant habits.

marching him to the outskirts of town, and hurling him into a river, but Baxter had gotten free somehow and come back that same night—wriggling through the mail slot, rolling up the stairs, and jumping on her chest, a filthy, sopping mess. In the end, giving the sentient ball of nightmares a name made its constant presence slightly less unsettling.

She'd been skipping school, but after a week she couldn't miss any more. She knew Baxter would follow her, and rather than try to explain her nightmare thread to teachers and classmates, she stuffed Baxter in a bag, slung him over her shoulder, and took him along. As long as she kept the bag near her, Baxter stayed quiet and didn't cause problems.

But Baxter wasn't her only problem. News of Lavinia's talent had circulated among the other students, and when the teacher wasn't looking, a fat-cheeked bully named Glen Farcus put a witch's hat made of paper on Lavinia's head.

"I think this belongs to you!" he said, all the boys laughing.

She tore it off and threw it on the floor. "I'm not a witch," she hissed. "I'm a *doctor*."

"Oh yeah?" he said. "Is that why you're sent away to learn about knitting while the boys all take science?"

The boys laughed so hard that the teacher lost her temper and made everyone copy from the dictionary. While they were silently working, Lavinia reached into her bag, pulled a single thread from Baxter, and whispered to it. The thread wriggled down the leg of her desk, across the floor, up Glen Farcus's chair, and into his ear.

He didn't notice. No one did. But the next day Glen came to school looking shaky and pale.

"What's the matter, Glen?" Lavinia asked him. "Did you have trouble sleeping last night?"

The boy's eyes widened. He excused himself from the room and didn't come back.

That evening, Lavinia and Douglas received word that their father would return the next day. Lavinia knew she had to find a way to hide Baxter from him, at least for a while. Using what she'd learned in her hated home economics class, she teased Baxter apart, knit him into a pair of stockings, and pulled him onto her legs. Though the stockings itched something awful, Father was unlikely to notice.

He returned the following afternoon, dusty and road-worn, and after he'd hugged both children, he sent Douglas away so he could speak with Lavinia in private.

"Have you been good?" her father asked her.

Suddenly and fiercely, Lavinia's legs began to itch. "Yes, Papa," she answered, scratching one foot with the other.

"Then I'm proud of you," said her father. "Especially because, before I left, I didn't give you a very good reason for why I didn't want you using your gift. But I think I can explain myself better now."

"Oh?" said Lavinia. She was terribly distracted; it was taking all her willpower and concentration not to double over and scratch her legs.

"Nightmares aren't the same as tumors and gangrenous limbs. They're unpleasant, to be sure, but sometimes unpleasant things can serve a purpose. Perhaps they weren't all meant to be removed."

"You think nightmares can be *good*?" said Lavinia. She had found a small bit of relief by rubbing one of her feet against the hard leg of a chair.

"Not good, exactly," said her father. "But I think some people deserve their nightmares, and some people don't—and how are you to know who's who?"

"I can just tell," said Lavinia.

"And if you're wrong?" said her father. "I know you're bright, Vinni, but nobody's that bright all the time."

"Then I can put them back."

Her father looked startled. "You can put the nightmares back?"

"Yes, I . . ." She nearly told him about Glen Farcus, then thought better of it. "I *think* I can."

He took a deep breath. "It's much too heavy a responsibility for someone your age. Promise me you won't try to do any of this again until you're older. *Much* older."

She was in such a torment of itching now that she was only half listening. "I promise!" she said, then bolted upstairs to pull off her stockings.

Locked in her room, she took off her dress and tore at the stockings—but they wouldn't come off. Baxter liked being bonded to her skin, and no matter how she pulled and pried, he wouldn't budge. She even tried using a letter opener, but its metal edge bent backward before it could separate Baxter from her skin even a tiny bit.

Finally, she lit a match and held it near her foot. Baxter squealed and squirmed.

"Don't make me do it!" she said, and held it closer.

Baxter reluctantly peeled off her and resumed spherical form.

"Bad Baxter!" she chastised him. "That was bad!"

Baxter flattened a bit, drooping with shame.

Lavinia flopped onto her bed, exhausted, and found herself thinking about something her father had said: that taking people's nightmares was a great responsibility. He was certainly right about that. Baxter was a handful already, and the more nightmares she took from people, the bigger he would grow. What was she going to do with him?

She sat up quickly, lit with a new idea. Some people deserved their nightmares, her father had said, and it occurred to her that just because she *took* them didn't mean she had to *keep* them. She could be the Robin Hood of dreams, relieving good people of their nightmares and giving them to the wicked—and as a bonus she wouldn't have a ball of nightmare thread following her around all the time!

Figuring out who the good people were was easy enough, but she would have to be careful about identifying the bad ones; she'd hate to give the wrong person nightmares. So she sat down and made a list of all the worst people in town. At the top was Mrs. Hennepin, the headmistress of the local orphanage, who was known to beat her charges with a riding crop. Second was Mr. Beatty, the butcher, who everyone said had gotten away with killing his wife. Next was Jimmy, the coach driver, who had run over blind Mr. Ferguson's guide dog while driving drunk. Then there were all the people who were simply rude or unpleasant, which was a much longer list, and the people Lavinia just didn't like, which was longer still.

"Baxter, heel!"

Baxter rolled over to where she was sitting.

"How would you like to help me with an important project?"

Baxter wriggled eagerly.

They began that night. Dressed all in black, Lavinia put Baxter in his bag and slung him across her back. When the clock struck midnight, they snuck out and went all over town giving nightmares to people on the list—the worst to those at the top, itty-bitty ones to those further down. Lavinia pulled strands from Baxter and sent them wriggling up drainpipes and through open windows toward their intended targets. By the night's end they had visited dozens of houses and Baxter had shrunk to the size of an apple—small enough to fit in Lavinia's pocket. She returned home exhausted, falling into a deep and happy sleep the moment her head touched her pillow.

After a few days, it became clear that there would be consequences for what Lavinia had done. She came downstairs to find her father sitting at the breakfast table, tut-tutting at his newspaper. Jimmy, the omnibus driver, had gotten into a terrible accident, so exhausted was he from lack of sleep. The next morning, Lavinia learned that Mrs. Hennepin, agitated by some unknown malady, had thrashed several of her orphans into a coma. The morning after that it was Mr. Beatty, the butcher who was rumored to have killed his wife. He had thrown himself off a bridge.

Racked by guilt, Lavinia swore off using her talent until she was older and could better trust her own judgment. People kept coming to her door, but she turned them all away—even the ones who appealed to her feelings with tearful stories.

"I'm not taking any new patients at this time," she told them. "Sorry."

But they kept coming, and she began to lose her patience.

"I don't care; go away!" she would shout, slamming the door in their faces.

It wasn't true—she *did* care—but that little act of cruelty was her armor against the infectious pain of others. She had to wall off her heart or risk doing more harm.

After a few weeks it seemed she had mastered her feelings. Then, late one night, there was a tap at her bedroom window. Pulling back the shade, she saw a young man standing in the moonlit grass. She had turned him away earlier that same day.

"Didn't I tell you to go away?" she said through the cracked window.

"I'm sorry," he said, "but I'm desperate. If you can't help me, perhaps you might know of someone else who can take away my nightmares. I'm afraid they will drive me mad."

She had hardly looked at the young man when she'd sent him away earlier, but there was something in his expression now that made her gaze linger. He had a gentle face and kind, soft eyes, but his clothes were dirty and his hair askew, as if he'd narrowly survived some trauma. Though the night was warm and dry, he was shaking.

She knew she should have closed her shades and sent him away again. Against her better judgment, she listened as the young man detailed the terrors that tormented his sleep: devils and monsters, succubi and incubi, scenes conjured straight from Hell. Just hearing about them gave Lavinia the shivers—and she was not someone who got the shivers easily. Yet she was not tempted to help him. She wanted no more troublesome nightmare thread, and so she told him that, as sorry as it made her, she couldn't help him. "Go home," she said. "It's late; your parents will worry."

The young man burst into tears. "No, they won't," he wept.

"Why not?" she asked, though she knew she shouldn't have. "Are they cruel? Do they mistreat you?"

"No," he said. "They're dead."

"Dead!" Lavinia said. Her own mother had died of scarlet fever when Lavinia was young, and it had been very hard—but to lose *both* parents! She could feel a gap widening in her armor.

"Perhaps I could bear it if they had died a peaceful death, but they did not," said the young man. "They were killed—murdered—right before my eyes. That's where all my terrible dreams came from."

Lavinia knew then that she was going to help him. If she had been born with this talent in order to free just one person from their nightmares, she thought, it had to be this young man. If that meant Baxter would become too large to hide, well, then she would just have to show Baxter to her father and admit what she had done. He would understand, she thought, when he heard the young man's story.

She invited him inside, laid him on her bed, and reeled out amazing lengths of black thread from his ear. He had more nightmares clogging his brain than anyone she'd treated, and when she had finished, thread covered her floor in a wide, squirming mat. The young man thanked her, flashed a strange smile, and slipped out her window so quickly he tore his shirt on the jamb.

An hour later, Lavinia was still puzzling over that smile when dawn broke. The new thread hadn't finished coalescing into ball form, and Baxter, who seemed frightened of it, cowered in her pocket.

Her father called the children to breakfast. Lavinia realized she wasn't quite ready to tell him what she'd done. It had been a long night, and she needed something to eat first. She swept the thread under her bed. She closed her bedroom door, locked it behind her, and went downstairs.

Her father was sitting at the table, engrossed in the newspaper.

"Awful," he muttered, shaking his head.

"What is it?" Lavinia asked.

He laid the paper down. "It's so depraved I hesitate even to tell you. But it happened not far from here, and I suppose you'll hear about it one way or another. A few weeks ago, a man and his wife were murdered in cold blood."

So the young man had been telling the truth. "Yes, I heard," Lavinia said.

"Well, that's not the worst part," said her father. "It seems the police have finally identified their chief suspect—the couple's adopted son. They're hunting him now."

Lavinia felt her head go light. "What did you say?"

"See for yourself."

Her father pushed the paper toward her across the table. Above the fold was a grainy likeness of the young man who had been in her room only hours earlier. Lavinia fell heavily into a chair and clung to the edge of the table as the room began to spin.

"Are you feeling all right?" asked her father.

Before she could answer, there came a loud bang from the direction of her bedroom. The new nightmare ball had finished forming, and now it wanted to be near her.

Thud. Thud.

"Douglas, are you playing tricks?" her father called out.

"I'm here," said Douglas, wandering out of the kitchen in his pajamas. "What's that noise?"

Lavinia raced to her room, removed the chair, and opened her door. The thread had indeed formed a sphere. This New Baxter was huge—nearly half her height and as wide as the doorway—and it was *mean*. It rolled around Lavinia in a tight circle, growling and sniffing, as if deciding whether or not to eat her. When her father came bounding upstairs, New Baxter leaped at him. Lavinia shot out her hand and managed to grab one of its threads, and using all her strength she managed to hold the creature back.

She yanked New Baxter into her room and slammed the door. Her heart hammered as she watched it eat her desk chair, discharging a pile of wood chips behind it in an excremental trail.

Oh, this was bad. This was *terrible*.

Not only was New Baxter like a rabid dog compared to Old Baxter—it was made not from the dreams of an innocent child but the nightmares of a rotten-souled murderer—but there was a killer on the loose, and thanks to her he was now free of fear and inhibition. If he killed again, it would be at least partly her fault. She couldn't just throw New Baxter in a fire and be rid of it. She had to put it back from whence it had come: inside the young man's head.

The idea frightened her. How would she find him? And when she did, what would stop him from killing her, too? She didn't know—all she knew was that she had to try.

She pulled a fat handful of threads from New Baxter and wound them around her arm like a leash. Then she yanked it across the room and through her open window. On the ground outside was a torn piece of the young man's shirt. She picked it up and gave it to New Baxter to sniff.

"Dinner," she said.

The result was instantaneous: New Baxter nearly pulled Lavinia's arm off, tugging her across the yard and then down the road by its leash. New Baxter chased the young man's scent trail for much of the day, leading Lavinia all through town in circles, then out the other side of it. They traveled down a rural road into the middle of nowhere. Finally, just as the sun was setting, they came upon a large, isolated building: Mrs. Hennepin's orphanage.

Smoke was pouring from the lower-floor windows. It was on fire.

Lavinia heard screams from the other side of the building. She ran around the corner, pulling New Baxter after her. Five orphans were at an upper-floor window, gasping for breath as smoke billowed around them. On the ground below stood the young man, laughing.

"What have you done!" Lavinia cried.

"This house of horrors is where I spent my formative years," he said. "Now I'm ridding the world of nightmares, just like you."

New Baxter strained toward the young man.

"Go get him!" Lavinia said, and dropped the leash.

New Baxter spun across the ground toward the young man—but instead of eating him, it leaped into the young man's arms and licked his face.

"Hey there, old friend!" the young man said, laughing. "I don't have time to play right now, but here—go fetch!"

He picked up a stick and threw it. New Baxter chased it straight into the burning building. Moments later there came an inhuman scream as New Baxter was consumed by flames.

Defenseless now, Lavinia tried to run, but the young man caught her, knocked her to the ground, and wrapped his hands around her throat.

"You're going to die now," he said calmly. "I owe you a great deal for removing those awful nightmares from my head, but I can't have you plotting to kill me."

Lavinia struggled for breath. She could feel herself blacking out.

Then something jerked inside her pants pocket.

Old Baxter.

She took him out and jammed him into the young man's ear. The young man pulled his hands away from Lavinia's throat and fumbled at his ear, but he was too late; Old Baxter had already wriggled inside his head.

The young man stared into the distance, as if reading something only he could see. Lavinia squirmed but still could not get away from him.

The young man looked down at her and smiled. "A clown, a few giant spiders, and a boogeyman under the bed." He laughed. "A child's dreams. How sweet—I shall enjoy these!" And he resumed strangling her.

She kneed the young man in the stomach, and for a moment he removed his hands from her throat. He then curled his hand into a fist, but before he could strike her, she said:

"Baxter, *heel!*"

And Baxter—old, faithful Baxter—exited the young man's head suddenly and violently, flying out of his ears, his eyes, and his mouth along with a gout of thick red blood. He fell backward, gurgling, and Lavinia sat up.

The children screamed for help.

Gathering her courage, Lavinia got up and ran inside the house. She choked on the thick smoke. Mrs. Hennepin lay dead on the sitting room floor, a pair of scissors jutting from her eye socket.

The door to the stairway was blocked by a wardrobe—the young man's doing, surely.

"Baxter, help me! *Push!*"

With Baxter's aid, Lavinia was able to knock the wardrobe out of the way and open the door, and then she ran up the stairs, out of the worst of the fire and smoke. One by one she carried the children from the house, covering their eyes as they passed Mrs. Hennepin. When they were all safe she collapsed on the lawn, half dead from burns and smoke inhalation.

She woke up days later in a hospital, her father and brother looking down at her.

"We're so proud of you," said her father. "You're a hero, Vinni."

They had a thousand questions for her—she could see it in their faces—but for now she would be spared answering them.

"You were thrashing and moaning in your sleep," said Douglas. "I think you were having a nightmare."

So she had been—and so she continued to for years afterward. She easily could have reached into her own head and taken them out, but she did not. Instead, Lavinia devoted herself to the study of the human mind, and against great odds went on to become one of the first female doctors of psychology in America. She founded a successful practice and helped many people, and though she often suspected nightmare thread was lurking in the ears of her patients, she never used her talent to get rid of it. There were, she had come to believe, better ways.

Editor's note:

This story is unusual for a number of reasons, most prominently its ending. The pacing and visuals of its final act have a distinctly modern feel, and I suspect that's because it's been tinkered with in the not-too-distant past. I was able to find an older, alternate ending in which the nightmare thread Lavinia removes from the young man rises up to consume her, like a whole-body version of the stockings she knits early in the tale. Unable to peel off this wriggling second skin, she flees from society, having become a nightmare herself. It's tragic and unfair, and I can see why some latter-day tale-teller chose to invent a new, more empowering ending.

Whichever ending you prefer, the moral remains more or less the same, and it, too, is unusual. It warns peculiar children that there are some talents that are simply too complex and dangerous to use, and are better left alone. In other words, being born with a certain ability does not mean we are obliged to use it, and in rare cases, we are obliged not to. All in all, this makes for a rather disheartening lesson—what peculiar child, having suffered through the challenges of peculiarhood, wants to hear that her ability is more curse than blessing? I'm certain that's why my own headmistress only read this to the older children, and why it remains one of the more obscure, if fascinating, tales.

—MN

The Locust

—◦—

here was once a hard-working immigrant from Norway named Edvard who went to America to seek his fortune. This was back in the days when only the eastern third of America had been settled by Europeans. Most of its western lands still belonged to the peoples that had roamed it since the last Ice Age. The fertile plains in the middle were known as the "Frontier"—a wild place of great opportunity and great risk—and this was where Edvard settled.

He had sold everything he owned in Norway, and with that money had bought land and farming equipment in a place known then as the Dakota Territory, where many other new arrivals from Norway had also settled. He built a simple house and established a small farm, and after a few years of hard work even prospered a little.

People in town told him he should find a wife and start a family. "You're a strapping young lad," they said. "It's the natural order of things!"

But Edvard resisted marrying. He loved his farm so much that he wasn't sure he had room in his heart to love a wife, too. He'd always felt love was impractical, that it got in the way of more important things. As a young man in Norway, Edvard had watched his best mate throw away what could have been a life of adventure and fortune when he fell in love with a girl who couldn't bear to leave her family in Norway. There was no money to be made in the old country, and now his old friend had a wife and children he could barely feed—sentenced to a life of compromise and deprivation—all thanks to a whim of his youthful heart.

And yet, as fate would have it, even Edvard met a girl he took a fancy to. He found room in his heart to love both his farm and a wife, and he married her. He thought he could not possibly be happier—that his tough little heart was now full to bursting—so when his wife asked him to give her a child, he resisted. How could he possibly love a farm, a wife, *and* a child? And yet, when Edvard's wife became pregnant, he was surprised by the joy that filled him, and looked forward to the birth with tremendous anticipation.

Nine months later, they welcomed a baby boy into the world. It was a difficult birth that left Edvard's wife weak and ailing. There was something wrong with the baby, too: its heart was so big that one side of its chest was noticeably larger than the other.

"Will he live?" Edvard asked the doctor.

"Time will tell," the doctor replied.

Unsatisfied, Edvard took his child to see old Erick, a healer who'd made a reputation for himself in the old country as an uncommonly wise man. He put his hands on the boy, and within moments his eyebrows shot up. "This boy is peculiar!" Erick exclaimed.

"So the doctor told me," said Edvard. "His heart is too large."

"It's more than just that," said Erick, "though precisely what's special about him may not manifest itself for years."[1]

"But will he live?" asked Edvard.

"Time will tell," Erick replied.

Edvard's son did live, but his wife only grew weaker, and finally she died. At first Edvard was devastated, and then he grew angry. He was angry with himself for allowing love to disrupt his plans for a practical life. Now he had a farm to work *and* an infant to care for—and no wife to help him! He was angry, too, at the child, for being strange and special and delicate, but especially for sending his wife to the grave on his way into the world. He knew this was not the child's fault, of course, and that being angry at an infant made no sense, but he couldn't help it. All the love he had unwisely allowed to blossom inside him had turned to bitterness, and now that it was there, lodged in him like a gallstone, he didn't know how to get rid of it.

He named the boy Ollie and raised him alone. He sent Ollie to school, where he learned English and other subjects Edvard knew little about. In some ways the boy was recognizably his son: he looked like Edvard and worked just as hard, tilling and plowing beside his father every hour that he wasn't at school or asleep, and never complaining. But in other ways the boy was a stranger. He spoke Norwegian with a flat American accent. He seemed to believe that the world had good things in store for him, a peculiarly American idea. Worst of all, the boy was enslaved to the whims of his too-large heart. He fell in love in an instant. By the age of seven he had proposed marriage to a classmate, a neighbor girl, and the young woman who played the organ at church, fifteen years

1. How Erick knew the boy was peculiar from a simple laying-on of hands isn't clear; it's possible he was himself peculiar, and his ability was detecting peculiarity in others, even latent or undeveloped talents.

his senior. If ever a bird should fall from the sky, Ollie would sniffle and cry over it for days. When he realized that the meat on his dinner plate came from animals, he refused to eat it ever again. The boy's insides were made of goo.

The real trouble with Ollie started when he was fourteen—the year the locusts came. No one in Dakota had seen anything like it before: swarms big enough to blot out the sun, miles wide, like a curse from God. People could not walk outdoors without crushing insects under their feet by the hundreds. The locusts ate everything green they could find, and when they ran out of grass they moved on to corn and wheat, and when that was gone they devoured wood and fiber and leather and roofs made of sod. They would strip the wool from sheep in the fields. One poor soul was caught in a swarm of them and had the clothes eaten off his back.[2]

It was a scourge that threatened to destroy the livelihood of every settler on the frontier, Edvard's included, and the settlers tried everything they could think of to combat it. They used fire and smoke and poison to try to drive the bugs away. They pushed heavy stone rollers over the ground to squash them. The town near Edvard's farm mandated that every person over the age of ten deliver thirty pounds of dead locusts to the dump every week, or be fined. Edvard threw himself into the task enthusiastically, but his son refused to kill a single locust. When Ollie walked outdoors, he even shuffled his feet so as not to accidentally squash one. It nearly drove his father to distraction.

---

2. Extraordinary locust plagues afflicted the American West throughout the eighteenth and nineteenth centuries. The largest ever recorded appeared in 1875, when a swarm of more than twelve trillion locusts, blanketing an area larger than California, devastated the plains.

"They've eaten all our crops!" Edvard shouted at him. "They're ruining our farm!"

"They're just hungry," his son replied. "They're not hurting us on purpose, so it isn't fair to hurt *them* on purpose."

"Fairness doesn't enter into it," Edvard said, straining to control his temper. "Sometimes in life you have to kill in order to survive."

"Not in this case," said Ollie. "Killing them hasn't done any good at all."

By this point, Edvard had gone completely red in the face. "Smash that locust!" he demanded, pointing at one on the ground.

"I will not!" Ollie said.

Edvard was livid. He slapped his disobedient son, and still he refused to kill them, so Edvard thrashed him with his belt and sent the boy to his room without supper. As he listened to Ollie crying through the wall, he stared out the window at a haze of locusts rising from his ruined fields and felt his heart hardening against his son.

Word spread among the settlers that Ollie had refused to kill locusts, and people got angry. The town fined his father. Ollie's classmates pinned him down and tried to make him eat one. People Ollie hardly knew hurled insults at him on the street. His father was so angry and embarrassed that he stopped speaking to his son. Suddenly, Ollie found himself with no friends and no one to talk to, and he became so lonely that one day he adopted a pet. It was the only living creature who would tolerate his presence: a locust. He named it Thor after the old Norse god and kept it hidden under his bed in a cigar box. He fed it dinner scraps and sugar water and talked to it late at night when he was supposed to be sleeping.

"It's not your fault everyone hates you," he whispered to Thor. "You were just doing what you were made to do."

"Chirp-churrup!" replied the locust, rubbing its wings together.

"Shhh!" Ollie said, and he slipped a few grains of rice into the box and closed it.

Ollie began to carry Thor with him everywhere he went. He grew very fond of the little insect, who perched on his shoulder and chirped when the sun shone and would hop about merrily when Ollie whistled a tune. Then one day his father discovered Thor's box. Enraged, he snatched the locust out, took it to the hearth, and threw it into the flames. There was a high-pitched whine and a quiet pop, and Thor was gone.

When Ollie cried for his dead friend, Edvard kicked him out.

"No one sheds tears for a locust in my house!" he shouted, and pushed his son outside.

Ollie spent the night shivering in the fields. The next morning, his father felt bad for being so harsh and went outside to find the boy, but instead he came upon a giant locust sleeping between rows of ruined wheat. Edvard recoiled in disgust. The creature was as big as a mastiff, with thighs like Christmas hams and antennae as long as riding crops. Edvard ran into the house to fetch his gun, but when he came back to shoot the thing, locusts swarmed around him and flew into the barrel of his rifle, clogging it. Then they swirled in the air before him and divided themselves into letters that spelled a word:

O-L-L-I-E

Edvard dropped his gun in shock and stared at the giant locust, which was now standing on its hind legs, as a human would. It didn't have black eyes, like locusts do, but blue ones, like Ollie's.

"No," Edvard said. "It's not possible!"

But then he noticed that the torn collar of his son's shirt was around the creature's neck, and a cuff of Ollie's pants was attached to its leg.

124

"Ollie?" he said tentatively. "Is that you?"

In what seemed to be a nod, the bug moved its head up and down.

Edvard's skin prickled strangely. He felt as if he were watching the scene from outside his body.

His son had turned into a locust.

"Can you speak?" Edvard asked.

Ollie rubbed his hind legs together and made a high-pitched noise, but it seemed that was the best he could do.

Edvard didn't know how to react. He was disgusted by the very sight of Ollie, but still—something had to be done for the boy. He didn't want everyone finding out, though, so rather than call the town doctor, who had a big mouth, he sent for wise old Erick.

Erick came hobbling out into the field to have a look. After his initial shock, he said, "It's just as I predicted. It took years, but he's finally manifesting his peculiar trait."

"Yes, obviously," said Edvard, "but why? And how can it be reversed?"

Erick consulted a tattered old book that he'd brought with him—a folk manual of peculiar conditions, which had passed down through generations of his family from a great-grandmother who had herself been peculiar.[3] "Ah, here we go," he said, licking his thumb to turn a page. "It says that when a person with a certain peculiar temperament and a large and generous heart no longer feels loved by his own kind, he'll take on the form of whatever creature he feels most connected to."

Erick gave Edvard a strange look that made Edvard feel ashamed.

---

3. This was mostly likely *Vitalis is Peculiaris*, a medical book written in half-invented Latin by an unknown quack physician of long ago. Some of the advice it gives is quite sound, but most is madness; the trick is telling the difference.

"The boy had a locust friend?"

"A pet, yes," said Edvard. "I threw it into the fire."

Erick clicked his tongue and shook his head. "Perhaps you were a bit hard on him."

"He's too soft for this world," Edvard grumbled, "but never mind. How do we *fix* him?"

"I don't need a book to tell me that," Erick said, closing the tattered volume. "You have to love him, Edvard."

Erick wished him good luck and left Edvard alone with the creature that was once his son. He stared at its long, papery wings and its awful mandibles, and he shuddered. How could he love such a thing? Still, he made an attempt, but he was filled with resentment and his efforts were not sincere. Instead of showing the boy kindness, Edvard spent all day lecturing him.

"Don't I love you, boy? Don't I feed you and give you a roof to sleep under? I had to give up school and go to work at the age of eight, but don't I let you bury your head in books and schoolwork to your heart's content? What do you call that, if not love? What more do I owe you, you entitled American brat?"

And so on. When night fell, Edvard couldn't bear to let Ollie into the house, so he made him a place to sleep in the barn and left a few table scraps in a pail for him to eat. Toughness makes a man, Edvard believed, and being soft on Ollie now would only encourage more of the weakhearted behavior that had turned him into a locust in the first place.

In the morning his son was gone. Edvard searched every inch of the barn and every row of his fields, but the boy was nowhere to be found. When he hadn't returned after three days, Edvard began to wonder if he'd taken the wrong approach with Ollie. He had stuck to his principles—but for what? He had driven away his only son. Now that Ollie was gone, Edvard realized how little his farm meant to him by comparison. But it was a lesson learned too late.

Edvard became so sad and sorry that he went into town and admitted to everyone what had happened. "I turned my son into a locust," he said, "and now I've lost everything."

No one believed him at first, so he asked old Erick to corroborate his story.

"It's true," Erick said to anyone who asked. "His son is an enormous locust. He's the size of a dog."

Edvard made the townspeople an offer. "My heart is like an old, shriveled apple," he said. "I can't help my son, but if anyone can love him enough to turn him back into a boy, I'll give you my farm."

This excited the townspeople tremendously. For such a rich prize, they said, they could make themselves love nearly anything. Of course, first they had to *find* the locust boy, so they set out in search parties and began to comb the roads and fields.

Ollie, who had super-sensitive locust ears, heard everything. He'd heard his father talking about him, he heard the footsteps of the people searching for him, and he wanted no part of it. He hid in the field of a neighboring farm with his new locust friends, and anytime someone came near, the locusts would swarm up and surround the person, creating a wall that gave Ollie time to escape. But a few days later, the locusts ran out of food and took to the sky to migrate elsewhere. Ollie tried to join them, but he was too big and too heavy to fly. Being unsentimental creatures, not a single locust stayed behind to keep Ollie company, and he was left alone again.

Without his friends to help protect him, it wasn't long before a group of boys was able to sneak up on Ollie while he was sleeping and capture him in a net. They were the same boys who had tormented Ollie at school. The oldest one slung Ollie over his shoulder as they skipped back to town, singing and celebrating. "We're going to turn him back into a boy, and then we'll get Edvard's whole farm!" They cheered. "We'll be rich!"

They kept Ollie in a cage in their house and waited. When, after a week, he stubbornly remained a locust, they switched tactics.

"Tell it you love it," the boys' mother suggested.

"I love you!" the youngest boy shouted through the bars of Ollie's cage, but he could hardly get the words out before he started laughing.

"At least keep a straight face when you say it," the older boy said, and then he gave it a try. "I love you, locust."

But Ollie wasn't paying attention. He had curled up in a corner and gone to sleep.

"Hey, I'm talking to you!" the boy shouted, and kicked the cage. "I LOVE YOU!"

But he did not, nor could he force himself to, and when Ollie began making locust shrieks all night, the family gave up and sold Ollie to their neighbor. He was an old hunter with no family and little experience in matters of the heart, and after a few feeble attempts to show the boy love, he abandoned the effort and sent Ollie outside to live with the hunting dogs. Ollie much preferred the dogs' company to the man's. He ate with them and slept alongside them in their doghouse, and though they were afraid of him at first, Ollie was so gentle and kind that they soon grew accustomed to him, and he became one of the pack. In fact, he felt so accepted by them that one day the hunter found he was missing a giant locust but had gained an extra-large dog.

128

The months Ollie spent as a dog were some of the happiest of his life. But then came hunting season, when the dogs were expected to work. On the first day, the hunter brought the pack out to a field of tall grass. He shouted a command and all the dogs began to run, barking, through the field. Ollie followed along, barking and making a fuss. It was good fun! Then, suddenly, he tripped over a goose in the grass. The goose leaped into the air and started to fly away, but before it could get anywhere there was a loud crack and it fell back to earth, dead. Ollie stared at its body in horror. A moment later, another dog trotted up to him and said, "What are you waiting for? Aren't you going to take it back to Master?"

"Of course not!" Ollie said.

"Suit yourself," said the dog, "but if Master finds out, he'll shoot you." And then he grasped the dead goose in his jaws and trotted away.

The next morning, Ollie was gone. He'd run away with the geese, chasing their V-shaped migration from the ground.

When Edvard heard that his son had been found and then lost again, he sank into a despair from which those who knew him worried he'd never emerge. He stopped leaving his house. He let all his fields lie fallow. If old Erick had not brought him food once a week, he may well have starved. But like the locust plague, Edvard's time of darkness eventually passed, and he began to tend his farm again and to turn up at the market in town and in his old pew in church on Sundays. And after a time he fell in love again and married, and he and his wife had a child, a girl they called Asgard.

Edvard was determined to love Asgard as he had failed to love Ollie, and as she grew up he did his best to keep his heart open. He let her love stray animals and cry over silly things, and he never scolded her for acting out of kindness. When she was eight years old, Edvard had a hard season. The crops failed and they had only turnips to eat. Then one day a flock of geese was passing overhead, and one of them left the formation and landed near Edvard's house. It was very large, nearly twice the size of a normal goose, and because it didn't seem afraid, Edvard was able to walk right up to it and grab it.

"You'll make a good dinner tonight!" Edvard said, and he carried the goose inside and locked it in a cage.

It had been weeks since they'd had meat on their dinner table, and Edvard's wife was excited. She stoked a fire and prepared the cooking pot while Edvard sharpened his carving knife. But when Asgard came into the kitchen and saw what was happening, she became upset.

"You can't kill it!" she cried. "It's a nice goose, and it didn't do anything to us! It isn't fair!"

"Fairness doesn't enter into it," Edvard told her. "In life, sometimes you have to kill in order to survive."

"But we *don't* have to kill it," she said. "We can eat turnip soup again tonight—I don't mind!"

And then she collapsed in front of the goose's cage and began to weep.

At another time in Edvard's life, he might have scolded his daughter and lectured her about the perils of softheartedness—but now he remembered his son.

"Oh, all right, we won't kill it," he said, kneeling down to comfort her.

Asgard stopped crying. "Thank you, Papa! May we keep it?"

"Only if it wants to stay," said Edvard. "It's a wild thing, so keeping it in a cage would be cruel."

He opened the cage. The goose waddled out and Asgard threw her arms around its neck.

"I love you, Mister Goose!"

"Waak!" the goose replied.

That night they ate turnip soup and went to bed with their stomachs grumbling, happy as could be.

The goose became Asgard's beloved pet. It slept in the barn, followed Asgard to school every morning, and sat honking on the schoolhouse roof all day while she was inside. She let everyone know the goose was her best friend and that no one was allowed to shoot it or make it into soup, and they let it be. Asgard made up fantastic stories about adventures she had with her goose, like the time she rode Goose to the moon so they could see what moon-cheese tasted like, and she regaled her parents with these tales at dinnertime. That's why they weren't terribly surprised when Asgard woke them up one morning in a state of excitement and announced that Goose had turned into a young man.

"Go back to sleep," Edvard said, yawning. "Even the rooster isn't awake yet!"

"I'm serious!" Asgard cried. "Come and see for yourself!" And she tugged her tired father out of bed by his arm.

Edvard nearly fainted when he got inside barn. There, standing in a nest of straw, was his long-lost son. Ollie was grown now, six feet tall with strong features and a stubbled chin. He wore a burlap sack around his waist that he'd found on the floor of the barn.

"See, I wasn't lying!" Asgard said, and she ran to Ollie and hugged him hard. "What are you doing, silly Goose?"

Ollie broke into a big smile. "Hello, Father," he said. "Did you miss me?"

"Very much," said Edvard. His heart hurt so much that he began to cry, and he went to his son and hugged him. *"I hope you can forgive me,"* he whispered.

"I did years ago," Ollie replied. "It just took some time to find my way back."

"Father?" said Asgard. "What's happening?"

Edvard let Ollie go, wiped his tears, and turned to his daughter. "This is your older brother," he said. "The one I told you about."

"Who turned into a bug?" she said, eyes growing wide. "And ran away?"

"The same," Ollie said, and put out his hand for Asgard to shake. "Pleased to meet you. I'm Ollie."

"No," she said, "you're Goose!" And she ignored Ollie's extended hand and hugged him again. "How'd you become a goose, anyway?"

Ollie hugged his sister back. "It's rather a long story," he said.

"Good!" said Asgard. "I love stories."

"He'll tell us over breakfast," said Edvard. "Won't you, son?"

Ollie grinned. "I'd love to."

Edvard took him by one hand and Asgard by the other, and they led him into the house. After Edvard's wife had recovered from the shock, they sat together and ate a breakfast of turnips on toast while Ollie told them all about his years as a goose. From that day forward he was a member of the family. Edvard loved his son unconditionally, and never again did Ollie lose his human form. And they lived happily ever after.

The Boy Who Could Hold Back the Sea

here was once a peculiar young man named Fergus who could harness the power of the currents and tides. This was in Ireland during its terrible famine. He might have used his talent to catch fish to eat, but he lived in a land-locked place far from the sea, and his power was of no use in rivers or lakes. He might have set off for the coast—he'd been there once as a young boy; that's how he knew what he could do—but his mother was too weak to travel, and Fergus couldn't leave her alone, he was all the family she had left. Fergus gave her every bit of food he could scrounge while he survived on sawdust and boiled shoe leather. But it was sickness that finally got her, not hunger, and in the end there was nothing to be done.

As she lay dying, his mother made him promise to leave for the coast as soon as she was in the ground. "With your talent, you'll be the best fisherman who ever lived, and you'll never have to go hungry again. But never tell anyone what you can do, son, or people will make your life hell." He promised he would do as she said, and the next day she died. Fergus buried her in the churchyard, threw his few possessions into a sack, and began his long walk to the sea. He walked for six days with one shoe and no food. He was starving, and all the people in the towns he passed along the way were starving, too. Some towns had been abandoned altogether, the farmers gone to seek better fortunes and fuller stomachs in America.

Finally, he reached the seaside, and a little town called Skelligeen where none of the houses looked empty and none of the people looked hungry. This he took as a sign that he'd come to the right place: if the people of Skelligeen were still around and well-fed, the fishing must be very good. Which was a lucky thing, because he didn't think he could go much longer without eating. He asked a man where he might find a fishing pole or a net, but the man told him he wouldn't find any such thing in Skelligeen. "We don't fish here," the man said. He seemed oddly proud of it, as if being a fisherman were something shameful.

"If you don't fish," Fergus said, "then how do you live?" Fergus hadn't noticed any signs of industry in his ramble around the town: no pens of livestock, no crops other than the same rotting potatoes he saw everywhere in Ireland.

"Our business is salvage," the man replied, and did not elaborate.

Fergus asked the man if he had anything to eat. "I'll work for it," he offered.

"What work could *you* possibly do?" the man said, looking the boy up and down. "I could use someone who can lift heavy boxes, but you're scrawny as a bird. I'll bet you don't weigh seventy pounds!"

"I may not be able to lift heavy boxes, but I can do something no one else can."

"And what's that?" said the man.

Fergus was about to tell him when he remembered the promise he'd made to his mother, and he muttered something vague and scurried away.

He decided to make a fishing line from the lace of his shoe and try to catch something. He stopped a plump-looking lady and asked her where he might find a good fishing spot.

"You needn't bother," the lady said. "All you'll catch from shore are poisonous puffer fish."

Fergus tried anyway, using a bit of stale bread for bait. He fished all day, but caught nothing—not even a poisonous puffer fish. Desperate, his stomach in terrible pain, he asked a man walking along the beach if someone might have a boat he could borrow.

"Then I could go a bit farther out to sea," said Fergus, "where perhaps the fish are more plentiful."

"You'll never make it," the man said. "The current will dash you to bits on the rocks!"

"Not me," Fergus said.

The man looked at him skeptically, about to turn his back. Fergus really didn't want to break his promise, but it was beginning to look like he'd starve to death unless he told someone about his talent. So he said, "I can control the current."

"Ha!" the man replied. "I've heard some whoppers in my time, but that tops them all."

"If I can prove it, will you give me something to eat?"

"Sure," the man said, amused. "I'll throw you a banquet!"

So the man and Fergus went down to the shoreline, where the tide was going out for the day. Fergus huffed and grunted and gritted his teeth, and with a great deal of effort he was able to bring the tide back in, the water rising from their ankles up to their knees in just a few minutes. The man was astounded, and very excited by what he'd seen. He brought Fergus back to his house and threw him a lavish banquet, just as he'd promised.

He invited all his neighbors, and while Fergus stuffed himself, his host told the townspeople how Fergus had brought in the tide.

They were very excited. Strangely excited. Almost *too* excited.

They began to crowd around him.

"Show us your tide-pulling trick!" a woman shouted at him.

"The boy needs his strength," the host said. "Let him eat first!"

When Fergus couldn't force himself to take another bite, he looked up from his plate and around the room. Stacked in every corner were crates and boxes, each filled to the top with different things: bottles of wine in one box, dried spices in another, rolls of fabric in another. To one side of Fergus's chair was a crate spilling over with dozens and dozens of hammers.

"Excuse me, but why do you need so many hammers?" Fergus asked.

"I'm in the salvage business," the man explained. "I found them washed up on the beach one morning."

"And the wine and rolls of fabric and dried spices?" Fergus said.

"Those too," the man replied. "Guess I'm just lucky!"

The other guests found this funny for some reason, and laughed. Fergus began to feel uncomfortable and, thanking his host for the fine meal, excused himself to go.

"But he can't leave without showing us his trick!" said one of the guests.

"It's late, he must be tired," said the host. "Let the boy sleep first!"

Fergus *was* tired, and the offer of a bed was more than he could resist. The man showed him to a cozy bedroom, and the moment Fergus's head hit the pillow he fell into a deep sleep.

In the middle of the night, he snapped suddenly awake to find

138

people in his room. They crowded around the bed and tore his blankets off. "You've slept enough!" they said. "It's time to do your trick!"

Fergus realized he'd made a mistake, and he should have snuck out the bedroom window and run away—or better yet, never revealed his talent in the first place. But it was too late for that now. The crowd dragged him out of bed and down to the shore, where they demanded he pull in the tide again. Fergus didn't like being forced to do things, but the more he resisted, the angrier they got. They weren't going to let him go until he did what they asked, and so, resolving to run away at the first opportunity, he pulled in the tide.

Water came rushing in. The people jumped and cheered. A bell began tolling out to sea. A bank of fog cleared, revealing the lights of a passing ship, which was being dragged toward land by the quickly shifting tide. When Fergus realized what was happening, he tried to push the tide back out again, but it was too late, and he watched in horror as the ship smashed to pieces against a cape of jagged rocks.

Dawn began to break. The ship's cargo washed ashore in crates and boxes, along with the bodies of the drowned crew. The townspeople divided the crates among them and started carrying them off. This is what they'd meant by "salvage"—they were wreckers, and drew passing ships toward the rocks with false lights and signals. They were thieves and murderers, and they had tricked Fergus into doing their evil work for them.[1]

Fergus broke free from them and tried to run, but a crowd blocked his escape.

---

1. There are many accounts of villainous persons making false lights in order to confuse and deliberately wreck ships, but this is the only mention anywhere, in history or folklore, of a peculiar's power being used for such purposes.

"You're not going anywhere!" they said. "There's another merchant ship passing tonight, and you're going to help us wreck that one, too!"

"I'd rather die!" Fergus shouted, and then he ran in a direction none of them had expected—toward the water. He splashed into the surf, grabbed a splintered plank from the wreckage, and began to paddle. The wreckers tried to catch him, but Fergus used his talent to make a wave that rolled in reverse, pushing him away from shore rather than toward it, and soon he was far beyond their grasp.

"Idiot!" they shouted after him. "You'll drown!"

But he didn't drown. He hung on to the plank for dear life, the wave carrying him past the rocks and far out to sea, into the deep, cold water where ships passed.

He waited, bobbing and shivering for hours, until a ship appeared on the horizon. Then he made another wave and rode it toward the ship, and when he got close he began to shout. The ship was very tall and he was afraid no one would notice him, but finally someone did. A rope was lowered, and Fergus was brought up onto the deck.

The ship was called the *Hannah*, and it was filled with people who were emigrating to America to escape Ireland's famine. They had sold everything they owned to buy their passage, and now they had nothing but their lives and the clothes on their backs. The captain was a cruel, greedy man named Shaw, and no sooner had Fergus been pulled from the ocean than Captain Shaw wanted to throw him back again.[2]

---

2. The *Hannah* is not fiction. It was a real ship—and now an infamous one—that sailed from the Irish port of Newry on April 3, 1849, under the command of an inexperienced captain named Curry Shaw. Just twenty-three at the time, he had already earned a reputation as a ruthless man, and was widely despised even before the terrible events that befell his vessel.

"We don't allow stowaways on this ship," he said. "Paying passengers only!"

"But I'm not a stowaway," Fergus pleaded. "I'm a rescue!"

"I say who's what around here," the captain growled, "and all I know is you haven't paid for a ticket."

"I'll work for my passage!" Fergus pleaded. "Please don't throw me back!"

"Work!" the captain said, laughing. "You've got arms like noodles and little chicken legs. What work could you possibly do?"

Though Fergus knew his facility with tides and currents could be of great help to a ship captain, he had learned his lesson back in Skelligeen, and kept his mouth shut about it. Instead he said, "I can work harder than any man here, and you'll never hear me complain, no matter what you make me do!"

"Is that so?" said the captain. "We'll see about that. Someone fetch the boy a scrub brush!"

The captain turned Fergus into his personal slave. Every day Fergus was forced to clean the captain's quarters, iron his clothes, shine his shoes, and bring him his meals, and when he was done with those things, he scrubbed the decks and emptied latrine buckets, which were heavy and sloshed onto his feet as he dumped them overboard. Fergus did more work than anyone else on the ship, but, true to his word, he never complained.

The work didn't bother him, but the problem of the ship's food supply did. The captain had taken on too many passengers and not enough provisions, and though Captain Shaw and his crew ate like kings, Fergus and the passengers were forced to subsist on crusts of stale bread and cups of broth that contained more mouse droppings than

141

meat. Even those nearly inedible rations were in short supply; however fast the *Hannah* sailed, there was hardly enough to last the voyage.

The weather grew unseasonably cold. One morning it began to snow, even though it was late spring. One of the passengers pointed out that the sun was not where it should be for a voyage headed west, toward America; instead, they seemed to be sailing north.

A group of passengers confronted the captain. "Where are we?" they said. "Is this really the way to America?"

"It's a shortcut," the captain assured them. "We'll be there in no time."

That afternoon Fergus saw icebergs floating in the distance. He was beginning to suspect they'd been duped, so that evening he listened outside the captain's door while pretending to scrub the hallway.

"Just another day or two and we should reach Pelt Island," he heard the captain say to his first mate. "We'll pick up a cargo of furs, deliver it to New York, and that alone should double our profits for the voyage!"

Fergus was furious. They weren't taking a shortcut to America at all! They were purposely veering off course, making the journey longer and almost guaranteeing the passengers would starve before they reached port!

Before Fergus could slip away, the captain's door flew open. He was caught.

"He's been spying!" the captain cried. "What did you hear?"

"Every last word!" Fergus said. "And when I tell the passengers what you've done, they're going to throw you overboard!"

The captain and first mate drew their cutlasses. But just as they were closing in on him, there was a terrible crash and what felt like an earthquake, and they were all thrown to the floor.

The captain and the first mate picked themselves up and rushed from the room, Fergus and his threat forgotten. The *Hannah* had struck an iceberg, and it was sinking fast. There was only one lifeboat, and before the passengers knew what was happening, Captain Shaw and his cowardly men had commandeered it for themselves. Desperate mothers cried out for the captain to take their children aboard, but, pistols in hand, his men threatened anyone who came near their lifeboat. And then the captain and his men were gone, and there were no more lifeboats, and Fergus and the passengers were alone on a sinking ship in the middle of an icy sea.[3]

The moon was high and bright, and in its light Fergus could see the iceberg they had hit. It wasn't far away, and it looked wide and flat enough to stand on. The ship was listing badly to one side but hadn't yet sunk, so Fergus summoned a current and pushed the broken *Hannah* until its side bumped against the iceberg's edge. The passengers helped one another onto the ice, the last of them leaving the ship just before it sank beneath the waves. They cheered and rejoiced, but their voices were drowned out as a wintry wind began to howl. It seemed they had traded a quick death by drowning for a protracted one by cold and starvation. They spent the night shivering on the ice, huddled together for a little warmth.

In the morning they woke to find a polar bear lurking close by. It was thin and wretched-looking. The people and the bear watched one another nervously, and then, after a few hours, the bear stood up and walked to the edge of the iceberg. He seemed to have heard something, and when Fergus followed him at a careful distance, he saw a big school

143

---

3. This, too, is verified by history: late on the night of April 27, the *Hannah* struck an iceberg, and Shaw fled with his crew in the only lifeboat.

of fish churning the water a few hundred yards away. There were thousands of them—more than enough to feed everyone, if only they could be reached!

The bear flopped into the water and swam out toward the fish. He was too weak to reach it, though, and soon clambered back onto the iceberg, miserable and exhausted.

Fergus knew what he had to do, even if it meant breaking the promise he'd made to his mother yet again. He raised his arms, clenched his fists, and made a current that directed the fish right toward their iceberg. Soon, fish by the hundreds were banging against it and flopping up onto the ice. The bear roared with excitement, vacuumed several into his mouth, then scooped up a pawload and ran off.

The people were overjoyed. Though they didn't care for the taste of raw fish, it was better than starving. Fergus had saved them! They lifted him above their heads, chanting his name, then ate until they could eat no more.

As it turned out, Fergus hadn't *quite* saved them. Though they now had enough fish to last them weeks, that afternoon the temperature dropped and a blizzard blew in. As they huddled together for warmth, full but freezing, they realized that without blankets they would not live to see the morning. It was just turning dark when they heard a growl from outside their circle. The bear had returned.

"What do you want?" Fergus said, leaping up to confront it. "You've got all the fish you can eat, so leave us alone!"

But the bear's attitude had changed. He didn't seem desperate or dangerous now, as he had when he was starving. In fact, he seemed grateful, and he seemed to understand that Fergus and the others were in trouble.

The bear padded forward, lay down next to them, and went to sleep. The people exchanged tentative looks. Fergus tiptoed to the bear, sat down, and leaned carefully against him. The bear's fur was luxuriously soft, and his body radiated heat. He didn't seem to mind Fergus leaning against him at all.

One by one, the people approached. The children and the elderly snuggled right against the bear, the women nestled next to them, and ringing the outside were the men. Miraculously, though some were toastier than others, everyone survived the night.

The next day, the bear and the people were eating fish when another iceberg came floating past. There were three polar bears on it, and when the people's bear saw them, he stood up and roared.

Hey, fellows! he seemed to say. *There's a boy here who can get us as many fish as we like. Come on over!*

The three bears dove into the water and swam right over.

"Oh, great," one of the men said. "Now there are *four* bears on our iceberg."

"Don't worry," Fergus replied. "There's plenty of fish for everyone. They won't bother us."

The bears spent the day feasting on fish, and when darkness fell, they slept together in a big pile, the people nestled among them. That night everyone was warm as could be—men, women, and children.

The following day, another three bears swam over from a passing iceberg, and the day after that, four more came. The people were starting to get nervous.

"Eleven bears are a lot of bears," a woman said to Fergus. "What happens when they run out of fish to eat?"

"I'll catch more," Fergus replied.

He spent all that day and the next one staring out to sea, watching for another school of fish to appear, but he didn't see any. Their supply of fish was nearly gone. Now even Fergus was starting to worry.

"We should have killed that bear when there was only the one," an old man grumbled. "Instead, that peculiar boy brought us ten more—and now look at the mess we're in!"

Fergus could feel the people beginning to turn on him. He wondered what would happen when the fish ran out. Perhaps they would feed *him* to the bears! That night they went to sleep in a contented and furry pile, but in the morning the people awoke to find eleven polar bears staring at them hungrily, having finished every last fish on the iceberg.

Fergus ran to the end of the iceberg and cast his gaze desperately out to sea. What he saw made his heart leap for joy—but it wasn't a school of fish. It was land! In the distance was a snowy island. Better still, Fergus could see smoke rising from it, which meant it was inhabited. There would be people there, and food. Forgetting the danger of the bears for a moment, Fergus ran back to tell everyone the news.

They were unimpressed. "What good is land if we get eaten before we can reach it?" a man said, and then a bear approached him, picked him up by one leg, and shook him, as if hoping a fish might fall out of his pockets. The man screamed, but before the frustrated bear could take a bite of him, a gunshot rang out.

Everyone turned to see a man in white furs holding a rifle. He fired a second time, right over the bear's head, and the bear dropped the dangling man and ran away. Then the rest of the bears ran away, too.

The man in furs had seen them through a spyglass from the island, he explained, and had come to rescue them. He gestured for the crowd to follow him, and brought them to a hidden cove in the iceberg where

146

a flotilla of small, sturdy rowboats was waiting. The crowd wept with gratitude as they were ushered onto the boats and rowed to safety.

Fergus was thankful, too, but as they crossed the water he grew nervous that someone would tell the rescuer about his talent. It was bad enough that so many people already knew what he could do. But no one said a word about him—or *to* him. In fact, most of the people wouldn't even meet his eyes, and those who did gave him nasty looks, as if they blamed him for all their misfortunes.

His mother had been right, Fergus thought bitterly. Sharing his secret had only ever caused him trouble. It made people see him as an object, a tool to be used when it suited them and then tossed away when he was no longer needed, and he resolved never, ever to share his talent again, no matter what.

The boats docked at a small harbor ringed by timber houses. Smoke rose from their chimneys and the smell of cooking food hung in the air. The promise of a hot meal by a warm hearth seemed tantalizingly close. The man in furs tied his boat and stepped out onto the dock. "Welcome to Pelt Island," he said.

With a sudden chill, Fergus realized where he'd heard that name before: it was the fur-trading island Captain Shaw had been trying to reach when they were wrecked on the iceberg. Before he'd quite wrapped his mind around this, he saw something on the dock that astounded him even more: a weather-beaten lifeboat with the word *Hannah* on the side.

The captain and his men had reached the island after all. *They were here.*

A moment later, someone else noticed the lifeboat. Word spread quickly through the crowd, and soon a mob of angry people was demanding to know where Captain Shaw and his men were.

"They left us to die!" a woman shouted.

"They threatened us with pistols when we tried to save our children!" a man cried.

"They made us eat mouse-dropping soup!" said a scrawny young boy.

The man dressed in furs tried to calm them down, but the people were bent on revenge. They snatched his rifle, stormed into town, and discovered Captain Shaw and his men in the tavern, drunk as skunks.

A savage fight erupted. The crowd fought the captain and his men with anything they could find: rocks, pieces of furniture, even flaming logs pulled from the hearth. They were outgunned but the captain and his men were badly outnumbered, and finally, beaten and decimated, they fled into the snowy hills above the town.

The passengers had won. Several of them had been killed, but they had settled the score with evil Captain Shaw, and they'd reached dry land and civilization in the bargain. There was much to celebrate—but their cries of victory were soon interrupted by cries for help.

A fire had broken out.

The man in furs came running. "You idiots set our town on fire!" he shouted at the crowd.

"Well, put it out, then!" replied an exhausted fighter.

"We can't!" the man said. "It's the fire station that's burning!"

They tried to help the fur traders fight the fire with buckets of seawater from the harbor, but there weren't enough buckets and the flames were spreading fast. In desperation, the crowd turned to Fergus for help.

"Can't you do something about this?" they begged him.

He tried to say no. He'd promised himself he would refuse. But when their pleas turned to threats, Fergus found himself in an impossible situation.

"Fine then," he said angrily. "Stand back."

Once everyone had retreated to high ground, Fergus used all his strength and power to summon a giant wave from the ocean. It crashed into the town and put out all the fires, but as the great surge of water retreated again, it lifted the houses from their foundations and took them along with it. The crowd watched in horror as the whole town was swept into the sea.

Fergus ran for his life. The crowd, furious, chased him through the streets and up into the hills, where he was finally able to evade them by hiding in a snowbank. When they had gone, he got out, frozen to the bone, and stumbled through the wilderness.

After a few hours, Fergus happened upon some men in the woods. It was the captain and his first mate. The captain leaned against the base of a tree, his shirt soaked with blood. He was dying.

Shaw laughed when he saw Fergus. "So they turned on you, too. I suppose that makes us brothers-in-arms."

"No, it doesn't," Fergus said. "I'm not like you. You're a monster."

"I'm just a man," the captain said. "It's *you* they consider a monster. And what people think of you is all that really matters."

"But all I've ever tried to do is help people!" said Fergus.

After he'd said it, though, he wondered if it was really true. The ungrateful crowd had been threatening him when he summoned a wave to douse the fires. Had he, in his anger, created a larger wave than was needed? Had a small, dark part of him destroyed the town on purpose?

Maybe he *was* a monster.

He decided the only thing to do was to seek a life of permanent

149

solitude. Fergus left the captain to die and walked down the hills toward the town. Night was falling as he slipped through the ruined streets, and no one saw him. He looked for a boat at the docks that he might use, but they had all been unmoored and scattered out to sea by the great wave.

He jumped in the water and swam out to something that appeared in the darkness to be a large, flipped-over boat, but it turned out to be one of the town's wooden houses, floating on its side. He crawled in through the front door, summoned a wave to right the house, and rode it out to sea, due south.

For days he pushed his houseboat farther and farther south, eating fish that flopped through the front door. After a week, he stopped seeing icebergs. After two the weather began to warm. After three weeks, the frost cleared from his windows, the seas grew calm, and a tropical breeze began to blow through the windows.

The house still had much of its furniture. During the day he sat in an easy chair and read books. When he wanted to sunbathe, he climbed out the window and lay on the roof. At night he got into bed and was lulled to sleep by the gentle rocking of the waves. He drifted for weeks, perfectly content with his new life of solitude.

Then one day he saw a ship on the horizon. He had no interest in meeting anyone new and tried to steer the house away from it, but the ship turned in his direction, sails billowing, and quickly overtook him.

It was a formidable-looking schooner with three masts, and it towered over the house. A rope ladder was tossed over the side. It seemed the ship wasn't going to leave him alone, and Fergus decided he may as well climb aboard, tell the crew he didn't need rescuing, and send them on their way. But when he topped the ladder and clambered onto the deck, he was surprised to find the deck empty save one person—a girl about his age. She had dark hair and brown skin, and she was giving Fergus a very hard look.

"What are you doing in a house in the middle of the ocean?" she asked him.

"Escaping from an island in the icy north," Fergus replied.

"And how did you keep the house afloat?" she asked suspiciously. "And get all this way without a sail?"

"Just lucky, I guess," Fergus said.

"That's ridiculous," said the girl. "Tell me the truth."

"I'm sorry," Fergus said, "but my mother told me never to talk about it."

The girl narrowed her eyes at him, as if considering whether or not to throw him overboard.

Fergus avoided her gaze and glanced nervously over her shoulder. "Where's the captain?" he asked.

"You're looking at her," the girl replied.

"Oh," said Fergus, unable to hide his surprise. "Well, where's your crew?"

"You're looking at them," she said.

Fergus could hardly believe it. "You mean to tell me you sailed this huge ship all the way from—"

"Cabo Verde," the girl said.

"—all the way from Cabo Verde—by *yourself*?"

"Yes, I did," the girl said.

"How?!"

"I'm sorry," she said, "but my mother told me never to talk about it." And then she turned her back on him and raised her arms, and a great wind blew up and billowed the sails.

She was smiling when she turned around again. "My name's Cesaria," she said, and put out her hand.

Fergus was stunned. He'd never met anyone like himself before. "N-nice to meet you," he stuttered, and shook her hand. "I'm Fergus."

"Hey, Fergus, your house is floating away!"

Fergus spun around to see the house drifting away from the ship. Then a rather large wave hit the house, and it tipped over and began to sink.

Fergus didn't mind. He'd already decided he didn't need the house anymore. In fact, it just might have been Fergus himself who made the wave that sunk the house.

"Well, I guess I'm stuck here," he said, and shrugged.

"That's okay with me," Cesaria said, and grinned.

"Excellent," Fergus said, and grinned back.

And the two peculiar children stood grinning at each other a long time, because they knew they had finally found someone to share their secrets with.

The Tale of Cuthbert

———•◦•———

nce upon a peculiar time, in a forest deep and ancient, there roamed a great many animals. There were rabbits and deer and foxes, just as there are in every forest, but there were animals of a less common sort, too, like stilt-legged grimbears and two-headed lynxes and talking emu-raffes. These peculiar animals were a favorite target of hunters, who loved to shoot them and mount them on walls and show them off to their hunter friends, but loved even more to sell them to zookeepers, who would lock them in cages and charge money to view them. Now, you might think it would be far better to be locked in a cage than to be shot and mounted on a wall, but peculiar creatures must roam free to be happy, and after a while the spirits of caged ones wither, and they begin to envy their wall-mounted friends.

This was an age when giants still roamed the earth, as they did in the long-ago *Aldinn* times, though they were few in number and diminishing.[1] And it just so happened that one of these giants lived near the

———————————

1. That is not to say giants disappeared altogether; they simply stopped walking the earth. Read the tale "Cocobolo" to learn what became of them.

forest, and he was very kind and spoke very softly and ate only plants. His name was Cuthbert. One day Cuthbert came into the forest to gather berries, and there saw a hunter hunting an emu-raffe. Being the kindly giant that he was, Cuthbert picked up the little 'raffe by the scruff of its long neck, and by standing up to his full height, on tiptoe, which he rarely did because it made all his old bones crackle, Cuthbert was able to reach up very high and deposit the emu-raffe on a mountaintop, well out of danger. Then, just for good measure, he squashed the hunter to jelly between his toes.

Word of Cuthbert's kindness spread throughout the forest, and soon peculiar animals were coming to him every day, asking to be lifted up to the mountaintop and out of danger. And Cuthbert said, "I'll protect you, little brothers and sisters. All I ask in return is that you talk to me and keep me company. There aren't many giants left in the world, and I get lonely from time to time."

And they said, "We will, Cuthbert, we will."

So every day Cuthbert saved more peculiar animals from the hunters, lifting them up to the mountain by the scruffs of their necks, until there was a whole peculiar menagerie up there. And the animals were happy there because they could finally live in peace, and Cuthbert was happy, too, because if he stood on his tiptoes and rested his chin on the top of the mountain he could talk to his new friends all he liked.

Then one morning a witch came to see Cuthbert. The giant was bathing in a little lake in the shadow of the mountain when she said to him, "I'm terribly sorry, but I've got to turn you into stone."

"Why would you do that?" asked the giant. "I'm very kindly. A helping sort of giant."

And she said, "I was hired by the family of the hunter you squashed."

"Ah," he replied. "Forgot about him."

"I'm terribly sorry," the witch said again, and then she waved a birch branch at him and poor Cuthbert turned to stone.

All of a sudden Cuthbert became very heavy—so heavy that he began to sink into the lake. He sank and sank and didn't stop sinking until he was covered in water all the way up to his neck. His animal friends saw what was happening, and though they felt terrible about it, they decided they could do nothing to help him.

"I know you can't save me," Cuthbert shouted up to his friends, "but at least come and talk to me! I'm stuck down here, and so very lonely!"

"But if we come down there the hunters will shoot us!" they called back.

Cuthbert knew they were right, but still he pleaded with them.

"Talk to me!" he cried. "Please come and talk to me!"

The animals tried singing and shouting to poor Cuthbert from the safety of their cliff-top, but they were too distant and their voices too small, so that even to Cuthbert and his giant ears they sounded quieter than the whisper of leaves in the wind.

"Talk to me!" he begged. "Come and talk to me!"

But they never did. And he was still crying when his throat turned to stone like the rest of him.

Editor's note:

That is, historically, where the tale ends. However, it's so terribly sad, so lacking in useful moral lessons, and so well-known for leaving listeners in tears, that it's become a tradition among tellers to improvise new and less dire conclusions. I've taken the liberty of including my own here.

—MN

The animals tried singing and shouting to poor Cuthbert from the safety of their cliff-top, but they were too distant and their voices too small, so that even to Cuthbert and his giant ears they sounded quieter than the whisper of leaves in the wind.

"Talk to me!" he begged. "Come and talk to me!"

After a while the animals began to feel very bad, especially the emu-raffe.

"Oh, for goodness' sake," he said. "All he wants is some company. Is that so much to ask?"

"I daresay it is," said the grimbear. "It's dangerous down there—and with Cuthbert turned to stone, how will we get back up to the safety of our cliff-top?"

"There's nothing that can be done for him," said the two-headed lynx. "Unless you know how to reverse a witch's curse."

"Of course I don't," said the emu-raffe, "but that doesn't matter. We're all going to die one day, and perhaps today it's Cuthbert's turn. But we mustn't let him die alone. I wouldn't be able to live with myself."

It was more guilt than the other animals could bear, and soon they had all decided to join the emu-raffe, despite the dangers that faced them on the ground. Led by the 'raffe, they made a ladder of their bodies, linking hands to ankles, and climbed down the cliff-face to the ground. How they would ever get back to safety again was a question for another time. They ran to Cuthbert and comforted him, and the giant wept with gratitude even while he was turning to stone.

As they talked with him, his voice grew quieter and quieter, his lips and throat petrifying until they could hardly move. Finally he became so quiet and still that the animals wondered if he had died. The emu-raffe pressed his head against Cuthbert's chest.

After a moment he said, "I can still hear his heart beating."

The wren who could turn into a woman perched on the rim of Cuthbert's ear and said, "Friend, can you hear us?"

And from his stony throat they heard, no louder than a puff of breeze: "Yes, friends."

They broke into a cheer! Cuthbert was still alive inside his skin of stone—and so he remained. The witch's curse had been strong, but not strong enough to petrify him through and through. The animals were now poor Cuthbert's caretakers, as he had once been theirs: they kept him company, gathered food and dropped it into his open mouth, and talked to him all day long. (His responses became more and more rare, but they knew he was alive from the beating of his heart.) And though the wingless among them had no way to reach the safety of their cliff-top, Cuthbert kept them safe another way. They slept inside his mouth at night, and if ever hunters came along, they would climb down his throat and make howling noises that terrified the humans. Cuthbert became their home and their refuge, and even though he could not move a muscle, he was happy as could be.

Many years later, Cuthbert's heart finally stopped beating. He died peacefully, surrounded by friends, a happy giant. The wren, who had grown up to become an ymbryne, decided they had become too numerous to continue living inside the stone giant, so she brought all the peculiar animals to a time loop she had made atop the cliff.[2] She put the entrance to the loop inside Cuthbert. That way he would never be forgotten, and every coming or going was a chance to say hello to their old friend. And whenever she or any of the animals passed through Cuthbert, they patted him on the shoulder and said, "Hello, friend." And if they stopped and listened carefully, and if the wind was blowing just right, it almost sounded like *hello*.

160

---

2. They reached the cliff-top via an ingenious rope-and-pulley system Miss Wren engineered herself.

The Man Who Bottled the Sun

---•◉•---

ou may have heard that there are regions in the far north where the sun doesn't rise at all in winter, while in summer it shines constantly, even at midnight.

It wasn't always so.

There was a time when Iceland got as much sunshine in the winter as Spain. Then a peculiar man named Jón Jónsson came along and changed everything.

Jón's parents knew he was special from an early age. When he was seven he caught a flu that made him want to sleep all day, but there were no curtains on the windows and his room was filled with sunlight. His mother laid him in bed and went out to fetch the shutters, which were made of wood and normally used only during winter storms. When she returned with them under her arm, the room was dark. She thought she was losing her mind: she could see the sun glinting against the window glass, but its rays stopped there; the room itself was mired in a moonless night's gloom. But there was a glow beneath her sleeping son's sheets, and peeling them back she found light leaking out between the fingers of Jón's closed hand.

Carefully, she pried his fingers open.

There was a blinding flash. In an instant the room was filled with sunlight.

Jón woke up, groggy and blinking.

"Jón dear," said his alarmed mother, "what did you do?"

"I turned off the light," he replied, and then he did it again: he reached out, and with a motion like catching a fly in the air, he scooped the light from the room, closed his fingers tightly around it, and went back to sleep.

Though Jón's parents found this amazing, his ability didn't change their lives. The family trade was shoe making, and they lived comfortably enough. What good could taking sunlight from the air do them? Sometimes Jón would use captured sunlight in place of lanterns at night—lantern oil was expensive, after all, and daylight was free—but to stop the light from escaping before night fell he had to keep his fist closed tightly around it all day, which tired his hand and made it hard to do much else. He tried stashing sunlight in wooden boxes and glass bottles and goatskin bags, but it was no good—after a few minutes it always leaked out. Impressive though it was, his ability didn't seem to have a practical application.

Jón Jónsson's parents died when he was still a young man. A sickness swept through their valley and took them very suddenly. They'd only been buried a day when a tax agent came knocking and told Jón that everything his parents owned belonged to the government. They owed a debt of unpaid taxes worth more than their entire estate, and Jón stood to inherit nothing. He cursed the agent and vowed to fight the decision, and even went to plead his case before their assembly at Þingvellir, but to no avail. After months of fruitless protest, he found himself homeless and penniless. He packed up what he could carry on his back and left, and another family moved into the house where he'd spent his youth.

Jón Jónsson spent the next few years drifting from place to place, finding work where he could. He cobbled shoes in Akureyri, gutted fish in Grundarfjörður, and drove sheep down from the highlands in fall. He didn't make friends easily or stay in one place long. Lodged in him like shrapnel was the conviction that he'd been wronged and was owed a great debt, and it filled him with a bitterness that came spilling out of him at the slightest provocation. He was as curmudgeonly and disagreeable as an old hermit.

One day he was working with a road gang clearing rocks from a lava field. Sitting alone during his lunch break, he was surprised when a strange man dressed in gray and covered with wiry hair popped up from behind a boulder.

"Are you Jón Jónsson?" asked the stranger.

"I am," Jón said. "And who might you be?"

"My name is Tyr, and I have a gift for you."

"And why would you give me a gift?" asked Jón. "I've never met you before."

"Never mind that," Tyr said. "Here it is." From behind his back he produced a small, black box made of obsidian. "It's yours if you want it. I have only one condition: if you should earn any money by use of it, give me ten percent."

It was finely crafted and quite beautiful, and Jón thought perhaps he could sell it. As to why Tyr couldn't simply sell the box himself, Jón guessed he was a criminal of some sort, and to show his face in a town would've been too dangerous.

"Five percent and you've got a deal," said Jón—not because ten percent was too much, but because he liked to feel he'd gotten the upper hand in every transaction.

"All right," said Tyr, and he handed over the box so quickly that Jón wished he'd demanded two and a half percent instead of five. Before he could renegotiate, Tyr had ducked behind the boulder again, and when Jón went to look for him, he saw only a puff of smoke lingering in the air.

Jón tucked the black box into his knapsack, and at the end of the workday, he went into the town of Egilsstaðir to try and sell it. He offered it first to Grímur Snorrisson, the jeweler, but Grímur didn't know what to make of it. "Obsidian's wonderful for making knives," the jeweler said, "but why would anyone carve a box from it?"

"I've no idea," said Jón, "but I'll sell it to you for ten crowns."

"You must be out of your mind!" said Grímur. "It isn't worth two."

Next he tried to sell it to Steffi Ólafsdóttir, the wealthiest woman in town, for eight crowns, but she told Jón to go jump in a volcano. In desperation he cut his price to five crowns and offered it to Sveinn Swansson, who dealt in rare and precious objects, but though Sveinn said he'd never seen anything like it, he claimed to be short on cash. "Would you take four?" Sveinn offered.

"I won't be swindled!" Jón declared, and he stalked off with the box wedged tightly under his arm.

The sun was setting as he trudged back to the simple boarding-house where he was staying. Because the stingy landlord had only given Jón a single candlestick to light his room at night, Jón used his old trick and swiped a bit of fading daylight. (He took it from behind a sheep pen where no one ever went; he didn't want anyone to see a strange patch of black hanging in the air and start asking questions.) He snuck up to his room with the light clenched tightly in his fist. He'd meant to wait until it was good and dark to release it, but after a few minutes there was a knock at his door. It was the landlord, wanting to know if Jón could come outside to help him round up a cow that had wandered into the wrong field.

Jón cursed his luck and hid his glowing hand behind his back. He didn't want to help, but it seemed bad policy to refuse the landlord.

"I'll be there in one minute," Jón said, and closing the door he looked around for somewhere to stash his daylight. If I'm quick, he thought, perhaps it won't have all leaked away by the time I return.

His eyes fell upon the obsidian box. Since no container was really secure, it seemed as good a place as any, so he stuffed in the light, replaced the box's lid, and went outside. When he returned a few minutes later and peeked inside the box, he was astounded to discover that none of the daylight had escaped.

"What's this!" he exclaimed, then realized he must have made a mistake. "Perhaps there was more light in here to begin with than I remember," he said. "Yes, that must be it."

Just to make certain, before he went to work the next morning, he took another handful of daylight from behind the sheep pen and stashed it in the box. When he returned in the evening, he found the box as full of light as it had been that morning. He was so unready for this that he let it slip through his fingers and it leaked out everywhere, filling his small room with daylight just as the sun was disappearing outside.

Jón leaped up and down, whooping for joy: "It's a miracle, it's a miracle!"

A moment later the landlord was banging on his door and shouting, "How many candles are you burning in there, Jónsson? Put them out before you catch the building on fire!"

"Why, I'm not burning any!" Jón replied, and started to laugh.

The landlord threw the door open and stomped into the room. He had no sooner entered than he backed stiffly out again, eyes wide. "What in heaven's going on?" he said, his voice odd and high.

"You're dreaming," Jón replied. "Better go back to bed."

"Yes, yes, back to bed," the landlord mumbled. "Quite right." And he shuffled away down the hall.

Jón closed his door and got to thinking. If this box could hold on to daylight securely, perhaps there was money to be made from it. First, though, he had to understand a few things. How much light could it hold, and how long could it be held on to? The next day, he set off to find out.

Jón Jónsson saddled his horse and rode up into the highlands. When he came to a barren place where there were no people around for miles, he began to gather as much daylight as he could and stuff it into his box. For three days he rode back and forth in neat rows, as if tilling a vast field, so as not to miss a single ray. He climbed peaks so he could pull light from highest reaches of the sky, leaving cones of darkness above him and acres of it behind in long, zagging stripes. From a distance it looked as if sections of the earth had simply been vacuumed up. It so confused the wild rams and foxes that lived there that they would lie down to sleep in the middle of the day. Birds would not fly through the unnaturally dark areas and made long detours to avoid them.

When Jón's box was stuffed to the lid and would hold no more, he rode back to Egilsstaðir to see about selling it. Certain he was about to become a rich man, Jón set up a tent in the town square and held a nighttime demonstration to show what his boxed daylight could do.

Hundreds of curious townspeople gathered to watch.

The demonstration did not go well. First, Jón tried to show how the contents of his mysterious black box could be used to light very small spaces, like an outhouse.

"Imagine the call of nature wakes you in the night," he explained to the crowd. "You're half asleep and trying to light a lamp-flame in pitch darkness just so you can stumble outside and use the commode. It's dangerous! But with my boxed light, you won't need a lamp anymore— you can keep your outhouse lit round the clock!"

He'd brought a small, wooden outhouse into the tent, and now he pinched a little daylight from his box, tossed it inside, and shut the door. For a few seconds the outhouse shone brilliantly, shafts of light radiating through the cracks and seams in its frame, and the audience oohed and applauded. But they began to laugh as, moments later, all the light leaked from the outhouse, leaving the commode dark. Meanwhile, a luminous balloon of daylight rose through the air to become trapped in a distant fold of the tent ceiling, where it glowed uselessly, high out of reach. In an attempt to make his accident look intentional, Jón tried to brighten the whole tent by tossing handfuls of light into corners, but in his hurry he tripped and spilled half the contents of his box. The light that escaped was so concentrated that it rendered several people temporarily blind. Pandemonium erupted, the crowd ran screaming for the exits, and the tent went up in flames. As if that weren't disastrous enough, the daylight then escaped into the general atmosphere and lit the night sky bright as day. It stayed like that for an entire week, during which time the people of Egilsstaðir developed insomnia and slept not a wink.

Needless to say, there was no demand for Jón's boxed daylight. The townspeople wished only to be rid of it—and him—and Jón was told in no uncertain terms that it was time for him to leave Egilsstaðir. He rode away in shame, sorely disappointed.

Jón Jónsson drifted about the countryside, taking work where he could find it. He nearly forgot about his box of daylight, which he'd tied shut with string and stashed at the bottom of his knapsack. One day he was tarring boats in Húsavík when Tyr popped out from behind a pile of fishing nets.

"How's it going with the box?" Tyr asked. "Got any money for me?"

"Not a farthing," Jón grumbled. "The box is useless. You can have it back."

"Keep it," Tyr said. "You may find a use for it yet."

"I doubt that," Jón said, and he put down his tarring brush to reach for the box. By the time he'd pulled it from his knapsack, though, Tyr was gone.

The obsidian box had brought him only bad luck. Not only had it gotten him banned from Egilsstaðir, but ever since he'd started carrying it with him, he hadn't been able to find more than a day's work anywhere. Jón considered throwing it into the sea or leaving it under a rock for some other fool to find, but he couldn't quite make himself do it. Just a few more days, Jón thought to himself. If I haven't found a use for it by then, I'll get rid of it.

Three days later, Jón was on the road between Húsavík and Akureyri when he met a fellow traveler.

"What news?" the man asked, as was the custom.

"The whale's turd is heavier than the puffin's," said Jón, which was an old Icelandic way of saying nothing much. "What news have you?"

"The farmers of Egilsstaðir are in dire straits," the man said. "It's the height of growing season, but their volcano's been acting up, spewing ash everywhere. The sun's been blocked for weeks. It's a real problem!"

"Is that so!" said Jón. "How interesting . . . I mean, how terrible!"

He bade the man good-bye and spurred his horse toward Egilsstaðir as fast as it would gallop. Approaching the town, he saw dark clouds of ash clogging the sky, shading the land in a dusky, early evening dimness at noon. The crops had begun to wilt in the fields.

When Jón arrived, the farmers were holding an emergency meeting in the town hall. "What are we to do?" one of them was saying. "If this ash doesn't clear soon we could lose our whole crop!"

"Perhaps I could be of help," Jón said, and they all turned to see him standing at the door, the obsidian box in his hand. The farmers remembered what he had done—how his sunlight had lit up the night for a whole week—and they tripped over one another to give him their money.

Jón rode around town on his horse, distributing sunlight to each ailing farm—enough to bathe the fields of paying customers in sunlight, but no more. Their crops were revived to health within a few days, despite the ash that continued to blanket the sky.

Then Jón ran out of sun, and he had make another trip into the highlands to harvest more. He was gone several days. By the time he returned, the light he'd sold the farmers had petered out, and they were growing anxious.

"We were worried that something had happened to you!" one of them said. "If you hadn't come back, I don't know what we would've done."

"Never fear!" Jón replied. "I'm back, and I've got the best sunlight money can buy."

He sold nearly all of it within a day. His pockets were bulging with money, and before long the farmer's fields were bursting with healthy potatoes, leeks, and cabbages. Demand was so high that he had to raise his prices. The farmers grumbled about this a little bit, but they seemed to understand; it was business. Then Jón had an idea, and he went to look for Tyr in the lava field where he'd first appeared. He found the strange man dozing behind a mossy boulder and woke him.

"Ah, it's my business partner!" said Tyr. "Have you got anything for me this time?"

"I certainly do," replied Jón, and he gave Tyr his five percent.

"My, my," said Tyr, marveling at the weight of the purse he'd been handed. "You've done well for yourself!"

"I'd do even better if you could get me another obsidian box," said Jón.

172

"That could be arranged," said Tyr, "but if I give you another, you'll have to give me ten percent of your profits, rather than five."

The higher commission meant Jón would earn a bit less on each transaction, but with two boxes he'd be able to do twice as much business. "You have a deal," he said.

Tyr smiled, disappeared in a puff of smoke, and returned a few minutes later with a new box, nearly identical to the first.

Jón made another trip into the highlands. He was able to harvest twice as much sunlight, and he left regions of darkness behind him so vast it looked as if a solar eclipse had occurred. He sold it all, went back to harvest more, and made a handsome profit. He bought the largest house in Egilsstaðir to live in and hired a pair of armed guards to watch over his growing pile of money. But just when it seemed to Jón like the world was finally beginning to repay the debt it owed him, the ash clouds over Egilsstaðir began to abate.

Day by day, the sun was breaking through, and as it did, demand for Jón's product dried up. It seemed his run of good luck had ended. He had only half a box of sunlight left, but it was selling so slowly that he didn't bother making the long trip to the highlands to harvest more.

Then Tyr paid him a visit. Jón was smoking a pipe in his most comfortable chair when the strange man walked into his sitting room unannounced, startling Jón half to death.

"You might try knocking!" said Jón, leaping out of his chair. "And how did you get past my bodyguard?"

"Never mind that," said Tyr. "I hear you've given up. It wasn't part of our agreement that you could simply stop when you felt like it. If you're not going to use them, you'll have to give me my boxes back."

"I'm not giving up," Jón said irritably. "No one's buying."

"You disappoint me," said Tyr. "I thought you wanted to be rich."

Jón looked around the room—the well-made furniture, the bearskin rugs, the roaring fire—and said, "I am rich."

Tyr laughed. "I mean really rich."

"Of course," said Jón, "but what am I supposed to do? The sun's back. People aren't going to pay for something that's shining down from the heavens for free."

"Why, certainly they are," said Tyr.

"Oh yes?" said Jón. "Have you some book of spells to cast? Some dark enchantment to cloud their minds?"

"Nothing of the sort," said Tyr. "All you need is the magic of advertising." And he sidled up close to Jón and whispered in his ear.

When he'd finished Jon said, "Do you think they'll really fall for that?"

Tyr shrugged. "Would it hurt you to find out?"

Armed with Tyr's advice, Jón made a secret arrangement with a few of the farmers. He paid them to continue using his sunshine even after the ash clouds dissipated, and to tell their friends how much they loved it. To make sure their sales pitches were effective, Jón hired Snorri Sturluson, a young writer who was just getting started in his career, to pen some convincing lines. Here are a few:

"Nothing outshines Jón Jónsson's boxed sunshine. It's even better than the real thing!"

"My crops have never been so healthy, and their yield is through the roof! Why, my vegetables almost look good enough to eat. Ha-ha-ha!"

"The trouble with natural sunshine is that it never seems to fall when you need it to. But with Jón Jónsson's boxed sunshine, I've made nature my slave!"

The campaign worked like a charm, and even after the ash clouds disappeared, the farmers of Egilsstaðir were still clamoring for Jón's sunlight. They used it even when the sun was shining, convinced that the additional brightness infused their crops with extra nutrients. Whether or not it was true, enough people believed it so that the farmers who used Jón's sunshine were able to charge a premium for their crops at market, while the reputations of those who didn't suffered. Their vegetables were eaten only by those who could not afford the more expensive "double-sunshine-fortified" ones.

Demand was so high that Jón began to have supply problems. In exchange for an even higher percentage of Jón's profits, Tyr gave him a third obsidian box, but now he was harvesting the highlands' sunshine faster than it would grow back. The places he'd grown accustomed to collecting it from had gone permanently dim, which forced Jón to venture deeper and deeper into the barren wilderness in search of light. He tried to use the increasing difficulty of harvest as a pretense for raising his prices again, but this time the farmers pushed back.

"Why are you going so deep into the highlands to make your harvest?" said Grettir "Blood-Axe" Thorsson, the farmers' designated negotiator. "If it's expensive for you to travel so far, why not make your harvest closer to Egilsstaðir? Then you won't have to raise your prices."

"Because the highlands are the only place I can go that're completely uninhabited," said Jón. "I can't take sunshine from where people live."

"Nonsense," said Blood-Axe. "There's a valley near Seyðisfjörður that's uninhabited, or nearly so, and it's only a half-day's ride from here."

"Nearly uninhabited isn't the same thing as uninhabited," said Jón. "I don't want to make enemies over this."

"You won't," Blood-Axe said. "It's only a couple of families, and if they have complaints, they can come talk to me. They know which side of the toast their halibut paste is smeared on, if you take my meaning."

Jón didn't take his meaning, but he gave up arguing regardless. He didn't want to make those exhausting trips into the highlands any more than the farmers wanted to pay more for their sunlight, and he didn't really care about the families—he just didn't want trouble. To make certain there was none, Blood-Axe went along with Jón for the harvest.

When they reached the valley, it was not as sparsely inhabited as Jón had been led to believe. There were about a dozen houses dotting a grassy basin two miles square. How would they react when Jón stripped away all their sunlight in the middle of a golden day?

He quickly found out; he'd only harvested an acre when people came running out of their houses, waving their arms in panic. Jón left off harvesting while Blood-Axe went to speak with them. At first there was shouting, but things soon calmed down—in part, Jón assumed, because Blood-Axe was a near-giant and carried an axe on each hip. After a few minutes, the people returned to their homes.

Blood-Axe walked back to where Jón sat astride his horse. "You may continue," he said.

"What did you say to them?" Jón asked.

"Let's just say they came away from our conversation a lot wiser and a little wealthier," said Blood-Axe, cracking his knuckles.

Within a few hours, Jón's boxes were nearly full. He had stripped the entire valley of its sunlight. Amid the gloom, the houses were visible now only by the hearth-flames that glinted orange in their windows; all else was black.

"We can't leave them like this, can we?" said Jón.

Blood-Axe had already turned his horse toward Egilsstaðir. Jón sighed and began to join him, but before he could leave a woman came running up with a crying child in her arms.

"Sir, I beg you!"

Jón pulled his horse's reins and looked down at her. "What's the matter?" he said.

"It's my boy, sir," said the woman. "He's terrified of the dark."

The weeping child could not have been more than two. Though his mother rocked him and kissed his head, he would not be consoled. Jón's heart—for he did have a small one—broke.

"Blood-Axe!"

Blood-Axe stopped to look back at him.

"Wait ten minutes for me."

Blood-Axe crossed his arms and grumbled. Jón pulled the woman and child up onto his horse and took them home, where he took a big scoop of light from his box and spread it into every corner of their house, enough to keep it lit for a whole month.

Blood-Axe made fun of him all the way back to Egilsstaðir. "Are you looking for a wife?" he said, laughing. "That one's married already!"

"I felt bad for them, that's all," said Jón.

"Well, don't," growled Blood-Axe. "You'll never hear a word of pity from them when we farmers have a bad harvest. They look out for themselves, and so should we."

* * *

Jón's pile of money grew so long as the crops in Egilsstaðir did, but finally the growing season came to an end. The farmers thanked Jón for his excellent sunlight, and told him they looked forward to buying it again in the spring, when they planted a new crop.

"And I look forward to selling it to you!" said Jón.

"What'll you do with all your free time until then?" Blood-Axe asked him.

"I thought I might go on holiday somewhere warm. Rome, perhaps?"

"I hear it's nice this time of year. And they're almost entirely free of plague now!"

But just as he was making plans to go, Tyr paid him another visit.

"Quitting again, are you?" said Tyr, walking into Jón's room while he was getting dressed one morning.

"Good God, man!" Jón shouted, and jumped behind his dressing screen. "You've got to stop doing that!"

"You're missing a golden opportunity," said Tyr. "Don't you want to be obscenely wealthy?"

Jón looked around his room, which was draped with silks and expensive furniture. Gold coins overflowed from a chest in the corner. "I am obscenely wealthy!" Jón said.

"You could be the richest man in Iceland, if you weren't such a quitter."

"I don't know what you're talking about," said Jón. "I already managed to sell them sunlight they could've had for free—but now that the growing season's done, they don't need sunlight at all, free or otherwise!"

"Haven't you learned anything?" said Tyr. "What they need is irrelevant. They only have to want it."

"But they don't want it."

"Not yet," said Tyr, "but we can fix that."

He sidled up to Jón and whispered in his ear. When Tyr had finished, Jón scratched his chin and said, "I don't know. I think it's going too far."

"Try it," Tyr shrugged. "If they don't buy it, you'll know you were right."

Jón went to see Blood-Axe later that day.

"Jónsson, what are you still doing here?" said Blood-Axe. "I thought you were on your way to Rome!"

"I had a brilliant notion and I just had to share it with you," said Jón, and he pitched him Tyr's idea. "Natural sunlight is messy and inefficient. It falls in places where it isn't wanted, at times it isn't wanted. Let's say your family is away on a hunting trip for a week. While you're gone the sun shines every day, but when you get back it's all clouds and depressing gray skies. What a waste! But if you were to let me harvest and distribute your sunlight, you would never miss a ray."

"You want to take the sunlight we already get and sell it back to us?" Blood-Axe said, and the big man broke out laughing. "You're funny, Jón Jónsson!"

"I can see you're not quite convinced yet, but hear me out," said Jón. "Since I won't have to travel anywhere to make my harvest, I can sell it more cheaply than growing-season sunlight. And there's another advantage, too: you aren't limited to buying whatever light would have fallen on your property naturally. Some people won't want to buy much light, or won't be able to—which means that others can buy more than their natural share. If you want double-strong sun warming your house every single day of winter, that can be arranged!"

This seemed to pique Blood-Axe's interest. The farmers, having enjoyed a lucrative harvest season, were flush with money and looking for interesting ways to spend it. He had only one reservation.

"What about people who can't afford to buy your sunlight?" asked Blood-Axe. "Not everyone in Egilsstaðir is as well-off as we farmers."

"Blood-Axe, you surprise me!" said Jón. "Have you suddenly grown a heart?"

Blood-Axe frowned. "I'm only asking."

"I suppose the town could subsidize some light for the poor, if you feel like paying more taxes," said Jón. "But just between you and me, I think the people who work hardest to make this town what it is—and are rightfully enjoying the fruits of their success—are just a bit more deserving than the indolent slobs who don't contribute. Why should this town's most precious natural resource be given away for free to its laziest residents? Don't those people have the same opportunities to succeed as the rest of us? If they don't have money to buy sunlight, they have no one to blame but themselves. Who knows, maybe they'll find living in darkness motivating."

Blood-Axe's eyes widened a little. "Why, if I didn't know better, Jón Jónsson, I'd swear you were running for parliament."

"Now you're the one who's being funny!" said Jón. "No, no, I'm just a humble businessman. So, do we have a deal?"

"I'll have to take it up with the farmers' union," said Blood-Axe, and he went away shaking his head and chuckling.

The farmers' union loved the idea. Before it could be implemented, though, the town elders had to vote on it. They were sharply divided, so the night before the vote, Jón visited the home of each elder and gave them purses filled with gold coins. They were received without objection, with one exception.

"I don't accept bribes," said Bjarni Bjarnason, the eldest elder.

"I wouldn't dream of offering you a bribe!" said Jón. "This bag of coins is part of my municipal leadership revenue-sharing initiative."

"Is that what you're calling it?" Bjarni said with an imperious sneer. "And I suppose it's coincidence that you happen to be implementing this the very night before we vote on your proposal?"

"Pure coincidence," said Jón, smiling innocently.

"I'm sure," said Bjarni. He looked like he'd eaten a sour piece of fruit.

Jón shifted the purse from one hand to another. "My, it gets heavy," said Jón, shaking his free hand as if it ached. "Gold, you know."

Bjarni's eyes darted to the Jón's coin purse. "You must think I have no morals at all," he said.

"Not at all, sir. I think you're as honorable as they come."

"Good—then get off my property!" Bjarni shouted. "And leave that under my elderberry bush on your way out," he whispered.

"Yes, sir," said Jón.

The measure passed unanimously, and right away Jón began harvesting Egilsstaðir's light and selling it back to its residents. The endeavor was sufficiently complex that he had to hire an assistant—someone to collect payments and keep track of who wanted how much light and where, while Jón spent his days scooping sunlight from the sky and distributing it to those who had paid him.

At first, prices were low enough that nearly everyone could afford sunlight, though Jón heard a lot of complaints from poorer folk that this new expense was stretching their wallets thin, despite the subsidies. But as the long, gray winter set in, the rich farmers decided they liked warm sunshine and lots of it, and found that if they used enough, falling snow wouldn't stick to the ground and they could even go outside in thin shirts and short pants. It was like winter wasn't even happening! Delighted, they proceeded to buy so much sunlight that they drove up the price, and suddenly there were people in Egilsstaðir who couldn't afford any sun at all.

The town was profoundly changed. Previously, it hadn't been easy to tell who in Egilsstaðir had money and who didn't. Its modest and practical houses all looked more or less the same (except for Jón's), and people didn't dress in a flashy way even if they had the means. But now the divide was plain as day—quite literally. The wealthy side of town was bathed in bright sun, while the poor side was entombed in a permanent midnight. Temperatures were so balmy on the light side that it seemed as if winter had skipped it altogether, and the farmers and their fami lies frolicked outdoors much of the day, playing summertime games like skull toss and goat flip. On the dark side, though, winter had doubled down: snow piled high on roofs and it grew so cold that people had to keep their hearth-fires burning all night or risk freezing to death in their sleep. After a few weeks, the sun-starved poor began to suffer from frostbite and chronic lethargy. Desperate denizens of the dark side were found lingering near the yards of the wealthy, trying to soak in rays that strayed into the public road. The daring ones went farther, sneaking onto private property to pilfer sun on the sly. The elders declared sun theft a crime, deputized a police force to crack down on it, and many were jailed, dragged away shouting that the sun belonged to everyone. Poor citizens with suntans were hauled in for questioning, and those who could not adequately explain their skin tone were jailed, too.

The poor did not suffer these indignities quietly. They complained to the elders. They demonstrated in front of the town hall. They marched in front of the jail. But the farmers had no interest in giving up their new creature comforts nor their winter-less winters. They were convinced that it was their right to use as much sunlight as they could afford to, and the elders, who were being supplied with sunlight at a great discount, took their side.

Privately, Jón Jónsson had mixed feelings about the situation. Things were certainly going well for him—his personal fortunes were soaring—but it wasn't so long ago that he himself would have been too poor to buy sunlight. He didn't really believe what he'd said about how the poor deserved to be poor and the rich deserved anything they could get their hands on—that had been Tyr's line—but he was amazed at how readily Blood-Axe and his friends had adopted it, and how they could allow one principle to replace every other moral impulse.

"Don't you feel even a little bit sorry for them?" Jón asked Blood-Axe one day.

"Not at all," he replied. "If the dark-dwellers don't like how we do things here, they're free to leave town."

And indeed, some of them did, but there were many who could not, and they grew more and more desperate as the freeze hardened and their appeals were ignored. Eventually, desperation soured into anger. The dark-dwellers, as the farmers who lived on the sunny side of town had taken to calling them, threw hard looks at Jón as they passed him in the street. He didn't feel safe walking through Egilsstaðir alone, and in addition to the guards he employed to watch over his money, he hired several more to follow him wherever he went. The additional security was expensive, so to compensate he raised the price of light, and an even larger swath of town was thrown into darkness. Blood-Axe bought the sun they could no longer afford and used it to light his many stables and even the bottom of his well.

"Why on earth do you need light inside your well?" Jón asked him.

"So I can see how much water I have without going to the trouble of lowering the bucket," Blood-Axe said.

That night an old woman on the dark side of town froze to death in her bed.

The demonstrations grew larger. The crowds got angrier. A man was overheard plotting to burn down the elders' town hall, and was hanged.

An emergency meeting was called between the farmers' union, the elders, and Jón Jónsson.

"We can't go on like this," said Bjarni Bjarnason. "Something has to be done."

183

"Jón Jónsson will have to lower the price of his sunlight, that's what," said Blood-Axe. "It's the only thing that will mollify the dark-dwellers."

"That isn't fair!" Jón protested. "No, the town is going to have to subsidize more light for those who can't afford it. Then they'll stop demonstrating and threatening me, and I won't have to employ so many bodyguards, and I'll be able to drop the price."

"Why should we give all that light away for free?" said one of the farmers. "What have the dark-dwellers done to deserve our charity, other than threaten to burn down the town hall?"

"I say we kick them all out," suggested Blood-Axe.

Bjarni shook his head. "If you turn them out of their homes, they might come back seeking revenge."

"Put them in prison, then," said the fishmonger. "All of them."

"Too expensive," said an elder.

"Kick them out and build a wall around the town," said Blood-Axe.

"That would be like putting ourselves in prison," said the fishmonger. "Why don't we just kill them instead? Save us all a lot of money and trouble."

"Don't be absurd!" said Blood-Axe. "Who would we sell our vegetables to?"

After much discussion it was decided that, whether he liked it or not, Jón would have to lower his prices until things in Egilsstaðir calmed down.

Jón was furious. "You can all choke on a herring!" he shouted, and stormed out.

Blood-Axe chased him outside. "Be reasonable!" he called after Jón.

Jón didn't look back. His six bodyguards escorted him home. He told them he didn't want any visitors, locked himself in his house, and paced from room to room, angry and brooding. He was reminded of how he'd felt as a boy when the taxing authority seized his inheritance and left him penniless. Why should he pay for the mistakes of others? It was the farmers who'd been reckless and greedy, not him! Not only was he being forced to slash his profits, but he was risking his safety to do it—after all, it was Jón Jónsson, not the farmers or elders, who had to venture into the dark section every week to strip away their dawning sun. How long before an attempt was made on his life? Even a dozen bodyguards couldn't guarantee his safety.

He decided then and there that he was leaving. He would take his long-delayed holiday to Rome, and sod the rest. See how well they managed without him!

He began to pack at once. He'd only tossed a few shirts into a case when there was a loud clap behind him and he spun around, startled, to find Tyr standing at the foot of his bed.

"Where do you think you're going?" he asked.

"Away from here," Jón said. "And don't bother trying to talk me out of it this time. The risk is no longer worth the reward. I quit!"

"I thought you wanted to be the richest man in all of Iceland," said Tyr.

"I am the richest man in all of Iceland, and what good has it done me? I work like a dog, I have no time to enjoy my money, and half this town wishes I were dead. I'm leaving first thing in the morning! Scratch that"—he tossed a pair of pants into his case—"I'm leaving tonight!"

"What about all your money?" asked Tyr, nodding toward a trunk in the corner that was overflowing with gold coins.

Jón stopped what he was doing and looked at the trunk. "I'm, er, taking that too, of course," he said, and Tyr watched in amusement as Jón tried to drag it toward the door. He'd only gotten a few feet before he had to stop to catch his breath.

"Fine," Jón panted, "point taken. I'll take as much as I can carry and hide the rest. But I'm still leaving tonight!"

He opened the trunk and began filling his pockets with gold. After a moment he stopped, looked curiously at Tyr, and said, "Well? Aren't you going to try and stop me, like you always do?"

"No," said Tyr. "They are."

He cocked a thumb at Jón's window.

"Who?" said Jón, and he looked out to see Blood-Axe and Bjarni Bjarnason at his gate, talking with several of his bodyguards. "What are they doing here?"

"It looks as if they're giving instructions," said Tyr.

"By what authority!" said Jón. "Those are my bodyguards!"

Out the window he saw Bjarni hand each of them a purse of coins. The bodyguards were nodding.

"Not anymore," said Tyr.

"Nonsense!" said Jón. "I'll pay them twice as much! I'm the richest man in Iceland, after all!"

"That may be, but you have no power."

"Yes I have!" Jón shouted. "I'll buy an army and flatten this whole rotten town!"

He kicked over his dressing stand and punched the wall, then stood quietly for a time, massaging his hurt knuckles and watching out the window. The guards had let Blood-Axe through the gate, and now he was leading them toward the house.

Tyr laid a hand gently on Jón's shoulder. "You're a prisoner," he said. "A very wealthy prisoner, but a prisoner nonetheless. And you'll have to do as you're told."

Slowly, Jón raised his eyes from the floor and looked at him. "Why have you come here tonight?" he said. "To watch the seeds of misery you sowed blossom? Well, I hope you're enjoying your handiwork. Three times I tried to quit, and three times you refused to let me — and now look what's happened!"

"I didn't force you to do anything. And I don't take any pleasure from your misfortune, Jón Jónsson, I truly don't."

"Then why are you here?" Jón demanded.

"I thought perhaps there's something you'd want to give me."

"Yes, a fat lip!" said Jón, and he swung his fist at Tyr.

Tyr dodged it easily—casually, even—then smiled. "No, something else."

Jón stared at him blankly for a moment, then realized what Tyr meant. "The boxes."

"Yes."

There was a loud bang on the bedroom door. "Jón Jónsson!" shouted Blood-Axe from the hall. "Come out at once. I want to talk with you!"

In a sudden rush, Jón dove under his bed and pulled out the obsidian boxes. "Without these, I'm of no use at all!" he said. "They can't force me to do anything!"

"Precisely," said Tyr.

"Will you keep them safe for me?" Jón asked him.

"Have no doubt," Tyr said.

There was more banging at the door "Don't make me break it down, Jón Jónsson!"

"Then take them," said Jón, pressing the boxes into Tyr's hands.

"What about your gold?" said Tyr. "When they find out you don't have their sunlight, they'll surely confiscate it. Perhaps I should keep that safe for you, too."

"But how will you carry it?" said Jón.

"Let me worry about that," said Tyr.

"That's it, Jón, I warned you!" shouted Blood-Axe, and there was a thud as the door shuddered in its frame.

"All right, just hurry!" Jón said to Tyr.

Tyr took off his gray cloak and threw it over the chest of gold. "Good-bye, Jón Jónsson!" he said with a smile, and then he, the chest of gold, and the obsidian boxes all disappeared in a great puff of smoke.

A moment later, the door came flying off its hinges.

Blood-Axe stumbled into the room with two guards.

"Thank goodness you're still here!" said Blood-Axe. "This man overheard you threatening to leave town!"

"Arrest me if you will, Blood-Axe, it won't make any difference," said Jón. "You'll never get another ray of my sunlight!"

"Why should I arrest you?" said Blood-Axe. "I just want to talk. Not that you're an easy man to talk to—I had to bribe your guards just to let me through the gate!"

"Well? What do you want?" said Jón.

"After you stormed out of the meeting, we had a change of heart," said Blood-Axe. "It was wrong of us to ask you to shoulder all the burden, Jón Jónsson, and we're ready to compromise."

"What? You mean . . . you're not making me your prisoner?"

"Are you feeling all right, friend? Where are you getting these outlandish ideas?"

In a flush of panic, Jón excused himself and ran out of the house to search for Tyr. All that night and the next day, he looked everywhere—every inch of the town, behind every rock in the lava field, even in the distant highlands—but the strange man was nowhere to be found. Jón realized he'd been had. Tyr had lied to him, and now both his fortune and the boxes that had helped him make it were gone.

Jón knew he could never show his face in Egilsstaðir again. He snuck away in the dead of night, disgraced and humiliated, with only his horse and the gold he had stuffed in his pockets. He rode and rode, crossing the whole frozen country, until he arrived in the valley where he'd grown up.

No one recognized him. He told them his name was Einar Eriksson. Using the gold he had left, he bought back the house his parents had built, and there he stayed for the rest of his days, earning his living as a shoemaker. He never again used his talent.

The town Jón Jónsson left behind was forever changed. Two days after he left, the last rays of sun over Egilsstaðir petered out, and the whole populace, rich and poor alike, were cast into darkness. They had not even the light of the moon to help them see, and when they eventually ran out of torches and candles and firewood, they had no way of seeing at all, and wandered the streets calling "Hey! Watch out!" and feeling blindly with their hands. No one could tell poor from rich any longer, and the townspeople were forced to band together in order to survive. Everyone in jail was pardoned. When they slept, the whole town crammed into the town hall so that their combined warmth kept them from freezing. Weeks later, when the sun appeared above the horizon at last, the people of Egilsstaðir had forgiven one another and agreed never to speak of Jón Jónsson or his cursed sunlight ever again.

That summer a crew of workers were clearing a road through the lava field when they happened upon three strange, black boxes hidden beneath a boulder. Curious, they opened them, and the heat that poured forth melted the men into puddles and spilled so much light into the sky that the sun did not set in the north of Iceland for the rest of June and much of July—nor the next summer, nor the next, and so it remains to this day. So it was Jón Jónsson, you see, who took the winter's sun and gave it to the summer.

Near the end of Jón Jónsson's life, when he was a very old man, Tyr appeared to him again. Jón was nearly blind by this time and did not recognize him.

"Are you Jón Jónsson?" asked Tyr.

"I haven't gone by that name in many years," Jón said. "And who might you be?"

"Why, it's your old friend, Tyr!" he said. "I have something for you!"

"I'm not interested," said Jón.

"Even if it might make you very rich?"

"Especially if it might make me rich," said Jón.

"Don't be daft!" said Tyr. "I owe you a debt, Jón Jónsson. Don't think I've forgotten about the gold I said I'd keep for you."

"You don't owe me anything," said Jón. "The debt is forgiven."

The moment he spoke those words, Tyr disappeared in a puff of smoke. Jón never saw him again, and he lived the rest of his days a free and happy man.

MILLARD NULLINGS is an accomplished philologist, a renowned scholar, and a former ward of Miss Peregrine's Home for Peculiar Children. While in residence there, he earned over twenty correspondence degrees, authored the world's most comprehensive history of a single day on a small island, and helped vanquish a couple of truly nasty monsters. He is allergic to grimbear dander and almond butter. He cannot be seen with the naked eye.

PENGUIN BOOKS

An imprint of Penguin Random House LLC
375 Hudson Street
New York, NY 10014

First published in the United States of America by Dutton Books,
an imprint of Penguin Random House LLC, 2016
Published by Penguin Books, an imprint of Penguin Random House LLC, 2017

Library of Congress Cataloging-in-Publication Data is available.

Penguin Books ISBN 9780399538544

Printed in the United States of America

5 7 9 10 8 6 4

Edited by Julie Strauss-Gabel
Creative direction by Deborah Kaplan
Design by Lindsey Andrews
Text set in Bulmer MT Pro
Drop cap images taken from *1000 Decorated Initials* from The Pepin Press
Additional images © Shutterstock

Photograph of Millard Nullings on page 191: Credit: Leah Gallo. 'MISS PEREGRINE'S
HOME FOR PECULIAR CHILDREN' © 2016 Twentieth Century Fox. All rights reserved.